The Witch of Mad Dog Hill

The Witch of Mad Dog Hill

And Other Strange Stories of the Sacandaga Valley

Don Bowman

Vaughn Ward, Editor

Bowman Books
Greenfield Review Press
Greenfield Center, New York

State of the Arts

NYSCA

Publication of this book has been made possible, in part, through a grant from the Literature Program of the New York State Council on the Arts.

ISBN 0-87886-143-2
Library of Congress Number: 99-76670

First Edition
Bowman Books #8
Bowman Books is an imprint of The Greenfield Review Press.
All of the volumes in this series are devoted to the contemporary tellings of traditional tales.

Design and composition by Sans Serif, Inc., Saline, Michigan

CONTENTS

III. WHITE HORSE FROM HELL

IV. A GHOST IS NEVER SEEN WITHOUT MITTENS

V. AUNT WILMA

FAITHFUL FRIENDS:
A FOREWORD

By Joseph Bruchac

Some years ago I entered into correspondence with Manly Wade Wellman, an author I still regard as one of the finest practitioners of what might be called American Gothic fiction. The most memorable for me of Wellman's wonderful stories, based in the mountains of Appalachia. can be found in his collection *Who Fears the Devil.* The stories feature a hero known as Silver John, a wandering musician who travels the remote valleys and hills collecting songs whose roots are both Elizabethan and eldritch. Invariably, his travels and those songs lead the hero into strange adventures.

Manly Wade Wellman, who was in his seventies when we began writing each other, was a terrific person to correspond with. He was as open to wonder as any of his characters and he discussed with me the folk beliefs that had inspired his tales, folk beliefs very similar to those of the people I knew from my own Adirondack mountains. In many ways, the Adirondacks are like a little pocket of what has become known as Appalachia. There, rugged folk of that same Scotch Irish stock have lived similarly independent lives high in the hills. Like their southern cousins, they have also often intermarried with Native Americans, usually Abenakis or Mohawks who, like the Cherokee of North Carolina, took to the hills to avoid being driven from their land.

I remember asking Mr. Wellman if he planned any further stories of Silver John. Were there any more such stories? Plenty, he wrote back. And not long after that the first of a series of delightful folk novels featuring Silver John began to appear, novels that he wrote near the end of his life to continue the tale he'd begun decades before, novels in which the Native American side of the heritage of Appalachia was made even more clear.

I cannot help thinking of my late friend Manly Wade Wellman when I consider the tales of the Sacandaga Valley told by another faithful and even more indefatigable elder correspondent, Don Bowman. A few years back I was priviliged to publish Don's first book, *Go Seek the Powwow on the Mountain*, stories from the Sacandaga Valley shortly after the turn of the century. Don collected those stories while he was with the crews that cleared the valley of people before the flood waters of the great dam covered their lost homeland. Most of those tales dealt with the Mohawk and Abenaki people who were pushed out of that valley when the dam came, people who befriended Don and allowed him to carry their memories.

Once again, in this newly-edited collection put together from just a few of the letters Don has written to me (and, as of this date continues to write!), you'll find reference to the Powwows, the Indian medicine men who practiced what Don calls "white magic." But you'll also encounter much more of the dark side of the supernatural in that lost valley—stories of those who had dealings with the devil, shape shifters, witches and plenty of haunted houses. Sacandaga had more than its share of ghosts.

As before, I found much that was familiar to me. As fertile as Don Bowman's imagination may be, he has always written about the things he was told and the things he saw and his memory is as sharp as an ax blade. A few names have been changed for obvious reasons, but the people and places in these stories are usually very real—and remembered by other old-timers. I've encountered more than one of my own relatives in Don's historically accurate memoirs. Folk lore, history and Don's creative eye intertwine continually through these tales written by a man who recognizes the dark side but always celebrates the light—without ever losing his sense of humor.

By the way, there are a few other little links between Don Bowman and Manly Wade Wellman. One of them is the way silver plays a part in the undoing of evil in their stories. Another is the character of Don Bowman himself, a first person narrator who winds through these yarns a bit like Silver John in Wellman's stories—though more of an active listener than a participant. And yet another is a certain little book that some might think is only a literary invention (like the *Necronomicon* of H.P. Lovecraft). Both Manly Wade Wellman and Don Bowman made frequent reference to that book, which Don calls *The Faithful Friend*. It is a collection of protective spells and folk recipes to dispel evil and practice some of that white magic certain of Don's Granny Ladies and Powwows kept so dear to their hearts. But *The Faithful Friend* is as real as the flood waters that filled the valley and covered all those doings recorded here with another layer of mystery. How do I know? I know because I still have my own copy of the book *Powwow, or the Faithful Friend* on the shelf in the old house where my grandparents raised me, less than twenty miles away from the Conklingville Dam.

But don't think that means I'm some kind of Powwow or white warlock myself. Like Mr. Wellman or Don Bowman, I prefer to do my magic with words on a page. Any ghosts or supernatural doings that we storytellers conjure up will only be in your mind's eye— mostly. And now here are Don Bowman's tales, suitable for those who want to do a little traveling through the dark. Enjoy the journey!

INTRODUCTION

By Vaughn Ward

Supernatural belief and custom were the order of the day.

-DON BOWMAN-

Culture is a set of stories we tell ourselves again and again.

-STARHAWK-

Nine or ten years ago I was working with Joe and Carol Bruchac on an Adirondack tall tale collection. "Joe," Carol said, "show Vaughn those letters. Maybe she'll have some ideas." The broken-down manila folder Joe produced -four or five inches thick and crammed with blue ballpoint or penciled letters on lined paper- was my introduction to Don Bowman, our garrulous Sacandaga Valley guru.

Folklorist that I am, the first words out of my mouth were, "Well, let's start by classifying them. We'll know where to go from there." Three years and two Adirondack folklore books later, Joe mailed me copies of the letters, typed and bound. There were lots of them: history and legend, humor and horror, personal anecdotes and contemporary commentary -all so woven into chatty, fascinating, serendipitous letters that I could not tell warp from weft. When the strands were all teased out, I'd found 425 separate narrative units: tall tales and jokes; supernatural lore; Native American teaching stories.

The Teller

A resourceful, independent, seventeen-year-old country kid when he went to work on the Sacandaga Valley demolition crew in 1927, Don Bowman already knew how to do a man's work. He was smart and curious and outgoing. In his words, "I listened and learned." He put it all down in notebooks. He held onto these stories, until, in retirement, he began sending letters and articles to people he hoped might be interested. In retrospect, Don Bowman knew he had helped demolish a world, a way of life. The Sacandaga Valley's own ancient mariner, Bowman is compelled to tell them over and over until we remember for him.

The Tales

Except for Don Bowman's exquisite localizations, Sacandaga Valley ghosts, witches and demons behave very much like their 15th and 17th century European and New England ancestors.

Bowman's accounts of valley denizens from other dimensions are close cousins to tales collected by Gardener, Jones, Thompson and Jagendorf in other parts of rural New York State at about the same time. Stories about devils in the form of black dogs, about nightmares (witches turning their victims into horses and riding them all night), about black sabbaths and slipskins and werewolves and the black cat's paw which, cut off, turns out to be the miller's aunt's hand, are well-traveled and more than twice-told. People talked - in the woods, after church, in the store. As time went on, tales of real local people or stories set in actual places were embellished with fragments from traveling legends about saints, sorcerers, and scholars.

Valley talkers had charms as old as fear itself, for baby, beast, and crops. Spells for managing malevolent entities and tips recognizing the Devil's many disguises were around for the asking. Sacandaga ghosts were helpful, interesting and funny in some cases; violent and vindictive in others; self-dramatizing or just plain wispy on occasion. Except for lovelorn suicides and that well-traveled, transparent, sunbonnet-wearing woman rocking on the porch, the vast majority of Bowman's ghosts were men. (Maybe the more mature female spirits were just glad, finally, to be able to rest!) Dutch Jake, attached as he is to the details of his wardrobe, is my favorite. The sinister, bottomless Big Vly, and Sacandag, the hungry river god—ghosts of a ravished place—are there in every telling.

These *legends,* traveling tales told or believed for true, were passed on to press home a lesson: Stay away from the strange old woman on the edge of town. Don't be seduced by beauty. Don't attempt to control the wild forces of nature. Don't be curious. Don't go parking (even in the horse-drawn buggy) with your sweetie. If you don't follow the rules, you'll disappear in the swamp or the beautiful girl you can't resist will be transformed to a tormenting hag. Stay within the circle of your own fire. Don't talk to strangers.

Granny Women, Powwows and Witches

By the time the notices that the valley was to be flooded arrived, descendants of 18th century settlers had intermarried with Abenakis and Mohawks, creating a hybrid culture and a barter economy stretching back five and more generations. Native shamanistic and herbal healing lore were overlaid with Mohawk Valley Palatine German power doctor traditions. Granny women descended from Europe's wise women practiced midwifery, healing, protection from spells. Some of them, for a price or a grudge, were also known to cast spells.

In those days before radio or penicillin or even that

many cars, before anyone except the "storekeep" and a few rich folks had telephones, country people carried on pretty much as they always had. And I mean always. Valley healers operated in a tradition so ancient they didn't always understand the words of their own incantations, passed *verbatim* for who knows how long, from who knows exactly where.

Curing and cursing motifs passed down to the 20th century are ancient and very nearly universal. Accounts of miraculous healings, as well as of maledictions, are part of mythology worldwide. For a very long time midwives, fortune tellers, traditional healers and even sorcerers were part of life, at court and in the country. Practices similar to ones used by Sacandaga Valley granny women and powwows appear to have been conducted by Egyptian magicians before the time of Moses!

In the late middle ages, scapegoating of midwives, eccentrics, psychics, widows, women too beautiful or smart for their own good, intellectual dissidents and the mentally ill was widespread. Healers—as well as Jews and Joan of Arc—were branded heretics, with the Church and the urban, male medical doctors the ruthless oppressors. By the witch hysteria's end, millions in the New World as well as the Old were executed in the name of righteousness. Most of the victims (some say 85%) were women.

A document commissioned in 1486 by Pope Innocent III and written by German monks Kramer and Sprenger, the *Maleus Maleficarum* or *The Hammer of Witches*, was the text for the European witch purges. Motifs from the document found their way into migrating tales and became the legacy both of 17th century New England settlers and of their Sacandaga Valley descendants. Here is part of what that document said:

> *For this must always be remembered, as a conclusion that by Witches we understand not only those*

which kill and torment, but all Diviners, Charm-
ers, Jugglers, all Wizards, commonly called wise
men and wise women and in the same number we
reckon all good Witches, which do no hurt but
good, which do not spoil and destroy, but save
and deliver. It were a thousand time better for the
land if all Witches, but especially the blessing
witch, might suffer death.

These projective, paranoid accusations made their
way into oral tradition. Occasionally, in one place or
another, often when there was a perceived threat to the
social fabric, the ghastly unreasoning erupted and ru-
ined lives one more time.

Disturbingly, more than 400 years after the Inquisi-
tion, a Sacandaga Valley granny woman was tried in a
general store's back room. The charges, all without actual evidence, were straight from the *Maleus Maleficarum* and the Salem witch trials. Don Bowman coun-
tered these assumptions with anecdotes from his own
experience and, in at least one case, tells us he was a
character witness for a woman charged with witchcraft—in the 20th century, not forty miles from where I
sit writing.

Scapegoating and ostracizing seem to be hard-wired
human responses. Many stories describe the good
wives, envious of younger, indepepndent, attractive
women, whispering about the *succubus* (a seductive female demon). Since an astounding number of social ills
seem always to have been blamed on poor single
women, needy widows were suspect. Widows who in-
herited their husband's property, on the other hand,
had more financial independence than other women
and were not subject to male control. Imagining these
non-conforming women to be evil emmisaries from another realm would have allowed people to rationalize
their fear and jealously. The old migrating tales were attached to these women and retold for true.

A friend, now in his 80's and a descendant of Lake Luzerne-Warrensburg area settlers, remembers going with his dad to see the covered bridge Osborn's Bridge was named for go under—to the accompaniment of political speeches and a festive local brass band. I asked him if he knew about any Sacandaga Valley witches.

> *Oh, yes. Every little hamlet had their own, you know. They'd tell fortunes and heal people. May Day, every little settlement had its own fair. The witches would set up booths and tell your fortune. When the dam came in, they all got together and put a curse on it. Said they'd fixed it so it would never hold. I think, when the dam held and the lake filled up, that's about when people stopped believing in 'em.*

Legends warning people how *not* to be are called *cautionary tales*. Sacandaga Valley variants remind us of their cousins: *Susanna and the Elders, Faust, Odysseus and the Sirens*, today's tabloids and yesterday's broadsides.

In the Sacandaga Valley, the word *powwow* referred to a Native shaman or healer, usually a man. Even though they practiced somewhat different traditions, it's likely that, by Mr. Bowman's day, most granny women and powwows were of mixed European and Indian ancestry. Bowman's accounts confirm what I've heard from local families conversant with this sort of thing. Both say the granny women and powwows learned from one another. Rather like contemporary specialists, each called on the other in a pinch.

Here and there, valley healing knowledge, and maybe a little magic as well, continue unbroken. The few people I know who still keep the old ways are descended from both New England settlers and Indians. Often they are active members of a Christian congregation as well. When I ask them where they learned, they will mention a grandparent, male or female, or sometimes a neighbor. The referent to Native powwows and witches mostly has gone the way of old Sacandag himself. However, as Don Bowman himself might say, who knows what lies buried under those deep waters?

The Flooding

The Great Sacandaga Reservoir was created in 1930 by order of the Hudson River Regulating District. In 1922, public reaction to three serious Upper Hudson River flash floods and subsequent epidemics overcame legislative resistance to a proposal first introduced in 1867. The state legislature voted to dam the Sacandaga River, a main tributary of the Upper Hudson. Although flood control was the publicly-stated reason, perusal of the list of businesses and municipalities among which the costs were apportioned suggests a subtext of interest among the powerful in harnessing the water power of the Sacandaga River : Henry Ford and Sons, Green Island; Adirondack Power and Light Company, Mechanicville; Hudson Valley Railway Company, Stillwater; United Paperboard Company, Northumberland; Union Bag and Paper Company, Glens Falls; International Paper Company, Glens Falls, among others.

It is impossible to avoid noticing that none of those with a vested interest in creating the Sacandaga Reservoir were valley residents. The Hudson River Regulating District took land and livelihood. It uprooted congregations where generations had been baptized and married. The reservoir inundated cranberry bogs, covered bridges, factories, schools, blacksmith shops, picnic spots, barbershops, crossroads stores, the Big Vly itself. 27,000 acres were annihilated, including the elaborate Sacandaga Park with its dance pavilion, amusement park and theater; the right of way for the Fonda, Johnstown and Gloversville Railroad; the villages of Conklingville, Day Center, Batchellerville, West Day, Beecher's Hollow, Fish House, Osborn Bridge, Benedict, Denton's Corners, Cranberry Creek, Mayfield and Musonville. Three Indian villages were sacrificed. Buildings not taken down and moved were abandoned, razed and burned.

Some saw the handwriting on the wall, fixed up their places and sold before the word about the dam got out. Others held on until the very last, even taking children to school in rowboats as the waters rose. Those whose property extended up the mountain, particularly on the north shore, were able to move to higher ground and maintain a subsistence living.

Displaced valley natives made their way to Amsterdam or Gloversville, Schenectady or Albany, Saratoga or Glens Falls, to try a hand at city life and indoor work. Others, older and lucky, found relatives elsewhere to take them in. The very plucky picked themselves up and started over. Some just didn't get over the loss enough to do much of anything for the rest of their lives. Some of their children aren't over it yet.

Known graves—or at least the headstones—were transburied to higher ground, but older valley natives say no one could have found and moved all the home burials. They say they saw coffin parts floating in the new reservoir. They say those disturbed spirits wander the lake to this day.

Of the original Hudson River Regulating District investors still in business, none uses water as a main power source.

The Way the Book is Put Together

The Witch of Mad Dog Hill is arranged in sections according to who told Bowman the stories.

The stories in *Aunt Millie and the Disappearances* are vignettes from Don Bowman's vivid, personal memories, often related to a particular place he was in the process of tearing down. *Sacandag* tales came from various men Bowman worked with on the demolition crew. Clayton Yates (who claimed as a young man to have been apprenticed to his aunt, a practicing witch) told the tales in *Aunt Wilma*. The legends and tales in *White Horse from Hell* and *A Ghost Is Never Seen without Mittens* have no specified tellers. They begin, as good tales always have, with, "I was told . . . ," or "and they said . . . " .

The Sources

I did a great deal of reading, trying to understand how these stories wound up in the Sacandaga Valley and what they might have meant to the people who told them. The books and articles I found useful for getting all this straight are listed in the bibliography.

There's not much in print about the Sacandaga Valley itself. *Go Seek the Powwow on the Mountain*, which I put together for Mr. Bowman in 1993, is the only written record we have that Indians lived in the valley at the time of its evacuation. In addition to Mr. Bowman's book and his articles in Sacandaga Valley newspapers, I know of three print sources:

> *The Great Sacandaga Lake*, a series of three historical pamphlets, published privately in 1990, 1991, and 1992 by L. Paul Masto. Now out of print, they are available in Sacandaga Valley libraries.

> "The Sacandaga Story," in *Saratoga County Heritage*, Violet B. Dunn, ed. Saratoga Springs, NY: Office of the County Historian, 1974.

> *The Sacandaga Story: A Valley of Yesteryear.* Schenectady, NY: Larry Hart, 1967. [Direct inquiries to Hart, The Daily Gazette, Maxon Road, Sche-

nectady, NY 12308.] In addition to Hart's excellent reporting, the old photographs help us understand what the place looked like.

Documents about the Sacandaga Valley and the Hudson River Regulating District are in archives and noncirculating collections at the Schenectady County Public Library; at the Office of the County Historian in Fulton and Saratoga Counties, New York, and at the New York State Archives of the New York State Library, Albany, New York. Files of stories, songs, and oral history from the Sacandaga Valley and surrounding regions, collected in the 1930's and 1940's by Albany Teachers' College students, are on deposit in the Harold Thompson Archive and the Louis C. Jones Archive in the Special Collections of the New York State Historical Association Library, Cooperstown, New York. Photographs, artifacts, and transcripts of interviews Town of Edinburg Municipal Historian which Priscilla Edwards and I conducted in 1983 with elderly survivors of the valley evacuation are at the Nellie Terrill Museum in Edinburg, New York. Photographs and other materials pertaining to the interviews are deposited at the Saratoga County Historical Society in Ballston Spa, New York, as part of the 1983–1985 Saratoga County Folklife and Oral History Project. These archives and collections are open by appointment.

My most helpful connection, appropriately enough, was a ghost:

In January, 1993, I was driving from my home in the Eastern Mohawk Valley to Cooperstown, in Otsego County, where I had permission to search the New York State Historical Association's archives for supernatural tales. Coming into town from Oneonta past the old motel, time collapsed between that blustery, bleak afternoon and another winter, twenty-plus years earlier, when my husband and I were students in the Cooperstown Graduate Program of American Folk Culture.

The late Dr. Louis C. Jones, my mentor and the founder of the graduate program, was on my mind. Before coming to Cooperstown where he made his name as a specialist in American folk art, "Uncle Lou "—as graduate students traditionally called him—taught folklore at Albany Teachers' College. A charter member of the New York Folklore Society, Dr. Jones was first known as an investigator of New York State supernatural lore. Turning between Riverbrink (the rambling, haunted estate where Lou and Aggie Jones lived when they were king and queen of the graduate program) and the stone house across the river (where they lived in retirement), I remembered yet another winter afternoon.

Maybe ten years before, my husband and I sat with Lou and Aggie in the stone house, enjoying the fire and their nurturing company. While Aggie finished dinner, Lou took us up the long, steep stairs to his study, lined floor to ceiling with books. When I expressed amazement that he had his own copy of *A Handbook of Irish Folklore,* Lou grabbed the maroon leather and boardbound volume off the shelf, scrawled in red ballpoint, "For Vaughn with love, Lou," right under the elegant, black, young man's script "Louis C. Jones, Fredericksted, St. Croix, 1946," and handed it to me across his massive desk.

"You'll use it," he said.

Now, driving down the back street along the lake, past the grand old Otesaga Hotel, the Farmer's Museum and the golf course to the NYSHA library lot, it seemed I should be getting ready to dash upstairs to class in the room on the left, across from the second floor stacks. Instead, I turned in the first door to the right, with its glass window marked "Special Collections." Laid out on the large oak library table was a pile of worn folders. I opened the one on top to find yellow, legal-size sheets of meticulously classified, red ink notes—in Uncle Lou's minuscule, calligraphic hand with those very tall capital letters! Slantwise, in the margins, he'd even noted titles of books he considered critical in understanding York State's demons, ghosts, and witches.

"You'll use it," it seemed I could hear him say.

List in hand, I made my way to the cellar stacks, where I spent hours going through shelves of old, rare volumes, including copies of the *Maleus Maleficarum, The Long Lost Friend*, Cotton and Increase Mather. Old and very long out of print, everything I'd worried about finding was there.

Uncle Lou, thanks for being there when I needed you.

Mr. Bowman, it's been a privilege.

PART ONE

THE LAST PRAYER

THE LAST PRAYER

He was an old man, real old. He came walking, using a cane in one hand for support. Lou and I were at work tearing the little, old, empty church apart. We were part of the demolition crew working on the dam project.

The old man stood in the little old buryin' ground next the church building. A huge white oak spread wide its branches. Our foreman, our boss man, had told us to always be nice to visitors, as some folks would come to see the last of what had been their homes and those of their parents before them before they were torn down, burned and the flood waters would rise to cover all.

"Be polite, answer any questions," he said. "Then tell them they must leave the valley."

So I threw up my hand and said the usual, "Nice day. Can we help you? You cannot stay hereabouts."

He, in turn, threw up his hand. "May I talk to you gentlemen for a few moments? Then I shall leave."

I looked at Lou. He nodded his head in agreement.

"Why sure," I answered. "We'll quit for our noonin' and share a bite with you, if you wish." I went over to the oak, picked up our two knapsacks with our lunches in and took them to a knocked down grave marker.

"Oh please, not there! Cannot we sit elsewhere?"

"Sure," said Lou. "Anywhere. But these stones will all be moved next week and the bones dug up and moved to some church yard away from high water mark."

3

So, we got a couple of boards we'd tore off the building and set them across some big timbers on the ground that were waiting for the Barn Burner Crew to come and torch to flames.

The old man hobbled over to a small gravemarker stone, which I'd noticed. It just had one word, "Dorothy" chipped in it. He ran his hand over the stone, took off his hat and stood silently as if in prayer. Lou looked at me, raised his eyebrows and shrugged his shoulders. In reply I silently lifted my shoulders. We'd seen sad people come before to the great 28 mile long valley. Our method was to keep still, let visitors talk or not. Some were silent, went off crying. Some got angry at us because we were the ones they could see and blame, not the big shots at some desk in far off Albany.

The old man came over. "Can I sit?" he said.

There was plenty of room. We waved him welcome to it. He sat down, thanking us. I extended a sandwich of fried bacon, partridge breast and dandelion leaves. I had my own little camp up on the side of one of the mountains that closed in the valley. Lou gave the old chap a cup of coffee from his thermos bottle, for I only drank water, even from my thermos. After a few bites to eat and a sip of coffee, he told us his name, which I'll not put down here.

Many years ago he had been sent to this little church to replace a parson who had died. It was winter and he arrived in a rented horse-drawn sleigh with a driver who helped him carry his belongings into the little parsonage next the church, the building we had already torn down. The driver helped him start a fire in the stove then returned to town, miles away. There were a couple coal oil lamps which they had lit and it made the place more cheery.

He cooked some food he had brought along and after eating, sat reading his Bible in the soft lamp light.

4

A knock came on the door. The parson responded and opened the door. A man's voice asked if he was the new minister and could he come in?

He was invited in. The man gave his name and said he was a carpenter from over Batchellerville way. He also served as undertaker taking care of dead bodies. He made pine box coffins.

Over a cup of coffee the carpenter-undertaker explained that there had been a fight in a grog shop. A woman was stabbed and had bled to death. The carpenter had moved the body to his shop, placed it in a coffin. With the help of his helper they'd placed the coffin in the sleigh.

They'd then driven the sleigh out to this remote cemetery to bury the body. The ground was frozen so hard and so deep they could not dig a grave, so they decided to leave the body in the basement of the parsonage and return in the morning to bury it. When the carpenter got home he'd heard that the new minister was seen going past in a sleigh to the church. So he had rushed to tell the parson that the coffin with the body was down in the cellar.

Well, that upset the parson. He thought that was no respect for the dead. And what about relatives? Wasn't there going to be a service, prayers and a viewing?

No! The woman had no local kin. She was a lady of ill repute, had even stolen money and things. She'd caused trouble among married couples and the lumberjacks and the rivermen held no deep love for her. Most everyone was glad to see her gone and would shed no tears for her. The carpenter said he would return with his helper in the morn. They would bring a half a stick of dynamite, blast a hole in the frozen earth of the graveyard and bury the coffin.

The minister sat down with his Good Book after the man left. He knelt to say some prayers for the poor departed soul of the woman in the lonely coffin below his floor. After a bit, he heard a knocking and a knocking. He started for the door, thinking the carpenter had returned. Then he realized the knocking was from below the floor. He heard a voice call out—also from below the floor, he thought.

Taking the lamp from the table he went to the corner of the room where the carpenter had pointed out a trap door. He lifted the trap and saw a flight of stairs in the lamplight. Lamp in hand he went down the stairs into the cellar. There on the beaten, earthen floor he saw the raw lumber of the coffin. All was silent; he couldn't believe what he had heard and decided it had been his imagination. But, just as he was about to leave he heard a scratching from inside the coffin. Quickly, lamp in hand, he went up the stairs and got the metal poker which was on the floor under the stove. Returning to the cellar with lamp and poker, he started to pry up the nailed-down lid of the coffin. Hands inside, he pushed and lifted off the lid. Inside he saw the woman that he was told was dead.

The person looked alive. She spoke and said, "Please pray for me. I have done wrong and the Devil is after me. Don't let him take my soul. Pray, pray for me!"

The old parson told Lou and I there in the graveyard that he had been very upset. He told us that he had placed his hand on the face and forehead of the woman. It did not feel like the cold marble of death. He knew a bad mistake had been made. He told the woman, "I shall not only pray for you, I shall go into the night and seek help. What is your name?"

"Dorothy," she answered. "No! Don't leave, just pray. Please!"

"Of course I prayed and as I soon as I said my prayers, I saw in the lamplight the pallor of death come over her face. Her arms stiffened. Still in prayer, I

6

touched her forehead again, laying my palm full on it. I felt her neck and her wrist. There was no pulse. Before she had seemed to be alive. But now she was dead. My prayers had stilled a tormented mind and soul. Hers was now the coldness in the flesh of one long dead. She was gone. Her soul was now with God. Her body was again ready for the grave.

"Leaving, I went back upstairs. I prayed long into the night, and my mind went in many directions. Finally I reached a decision. If I told my story, who would believe me? What good could come of it? My prayers had soothed the poor tormented soul. God Rest Her!

"Taking the lamp I again went into the cellar. I replaced the cover on the coffin with a prayer, and nailed it shut, with the poker. I knew God had won over the Devil in the cold cellar on that cold winter night. Again I prayed at the coffin. I then went upstairs, closed the trap door and rekindled the fire as the place had grown cold. I made coffee and soon the winter dawn came upon the land. The carpenter and his helper came in their sleigh.

"They blasted a hole in the earth. The coffin was carried out, placed in the grave. I said a few more prayers as the Sacandaga wind brought another snowstorm. The two men filled in the grave with frozen chunks of dirt. They left in the sleigh.

The local people accepted me as their new pastor. We got along very well. When spring came I had a headstone marked "Dorothy" placed on her grave, at my own expense.

"Thank you gentlemen for the lunch and for being the first and last to hear my story. I have a long trip ahead of me. Thank you again! I shall now give her my Last Prayer. May she be with God!"

He went and stood with clasped hands at the gravestone. Then he went limping away with his cane. We waved so long.

7

Lou and I thought it was a strange story and probably true, for it had brought him back over the years and miles to that simple, yet wonderful headstone that read "Dorothy." I know he too must now be with his God!

RETURN OF A WITCH

Lou and I had just torn down a barn at the old place. We were just starting to demolish the house when a car drove up and an old lady got out. She said her name was Rita—and wondered if she could see the inside of the house one last time? We told her "Sure." The boss had told us to be nice to any folks that came to look at places, because they had memories.

She looked around the empty house, then came out. She offered us a tip which we refused. Then she beckoned to the man who had driven the car. He came over with a peck basket of fine looking apples, told us to help ourselves. We did, apples tasted mighty refreshing. We all sat down on a pile of lumber from the barn, eating apples.

She told us that she had been the oldest of fifteen kids and she took care of all of them. The old man was mostly drunk and often beat up on her maw and the kids. Her maw was always having a baby. When Maw said number sixteen was on the way, Rita wrapped her few things in a brown paper sack and took off. She told us she saw and did many things. Some good, some bad, a few were even evil. In jail she met a woman who was even worse. She had killed a man and was never sorry for that.

The woman told Rita of the valley back in the mountains. Said Rita could go there, use the house and farm she owned. As far as she knew it was empty. Rita could go there and stay as long as she lived. If the woman ever got out of jail she'd return to the farm. They'd both live there together, each for their own life.

9

Rita came to the farm. She told folks at the store who she was and where she was gonna live and paid up the taxes. Folks asked no questions. It seemed as though some had their own past not to be talked about. Rita had a little money and she knew about babies. Maw had had plenty for Rita to learn on. She knew how to care for the sick and ill and fix men up after drunken fights and accidents of all kinds. She knew about herbs and roots, so she became a granny woman.

She paid a man to fix up the house, bought old furniture from some nearby folks she met and settled in the old house. The man put in a garden for her. She bought goats for milk and cheese and had a couple of pigs, some chickens and rabbits.

Folks seemed to think she was also a witch woman for her treatments did cure and heal some folks that came to her. So Rita bought a horse and carriage and visited known witch women up and down the river. Since she had some money she paid some of the women to teach her some witchery.

Her friend from prison, Lucy, got out and returned to the valley. She used to be a glove maker, so she worked at that. The two women got along well. Then Lucy got to drinking and ended up with a fight with another woman over some no-account lumberjacks—in a gin mill. Lucy got hit, fell down, hit her head and died the next day in the hospital over in Gloversville.

Rita kept on living at the house. Then the state came along with plans to make a dam and flood the valley. They were going to buy all the land. Rita had no deed to the property. The state marked her down as a "Squatter," but said that she'd been living there long enough to have what was called "Adverse Possession" of the property. She signed a Quit Claim Deed and was paid money in value for the place. She couldn't move the house as she owned no other land to move it on to. So she just sold her goats, chickens, pigs rabbits to dealers that came around, and she left, even sold the furniture.

She read in a newspaper that former people of the valley could return in a certain week to take a last look at the homes to be torn down. She had been ill, recovered, got a friend to drive her up from Albany for one last look at the only real home that she ever had had.

She thanked us and blessed us, left us the apples. The man helped her into the car. They waved goodbyes at us which we returned.

And that's the story of the witch that returned to Girdletree Farm!

Note:

The name Girdletree Farm went back a good many years. Many early settlers of the valley took unto them the best land. If there were trees they usually felled them with crosscut saw and axe. Used the logs. The stumps they dug up or burned, to make cleared fields and pasture lands.

A few properties the owners did not cut down at once. They girdled the trees, by cutting out a circle of wood and bark all around the tree. That cut off the sap. The tree died but remained standing for years. Planting and pasture was among the dead trees. In time they lost their bark, stood like gray ghosts of a dead forest.

11

OLGA THE WITCH-LADY

I was drivin' a team in a lumber camp. The cutting was hardwood logs meant for bridge timbers, ash bolts for baseball bats, yellow birch called silver birch for a plywood and panel factory. We also harvested soft woods, cut and bark peeled for the IP Mill at Corinth, poplar, pine, spruce, and tamarack. Later the mill put in a barking drum that took hard and soft wood with the bark on.

At the camp one of the choppers was Joe Petrowski, part Polish and part Russian. He spoke with a heavy accent with just enough English to get along. There were several other choppers of mid European blood. I used to be given the stamps off their mail. Payday night, the boss man who lived near Saratoga used to take some of the jacks in his truck to Saratoga, those who wanted to go. There they were on their own til Monday morn when they met the truck at the R.R. station.

Of course some of the men who were youngish, strong, active, full of vim and vigor found their way to famous Congress Street with the "cribs" where there was sex and drinks at a price. Joe had become friends with young Frank Kopiar at camp. His dad had a small farm just outside of South Corinth. Joe and Frank both became involved with two pretty girls at the Cribs. Joe had come from Europe on a pulp-wood ship from across the Atlantic. That wood was shipped from Russia or Finland on a sort of exchange fair trade—you buy from me, I buy from you. One very pretty girl named Olga had come over as a deck hand on a ship to

12

the Port of Albany and wound up in Saratoga in a Congress Street crib. Joe wanted her for himself.

Frank lost his heart to a girl named Ann, who was part Indian. She was brought from Pennsylvania to Saratoga by the ones who drove the girls to the Pennsylvania-York State line. Those girls would get out of the cars and walk across the state lines. Over in York State a transporter car with New York tags picked up the girls again and delivered them to Albany, Troy, Saratoga. That was to avoid arrest for transporting women across state lines under the Mann Act—White Slavery. Ann had a hawk nose, but was otherwise a very pretty girl with long black hair that shone like a crow's wing in sunlight. Frank fell for her like a load of cordwood.

When Frank wasn't working on the mountain he lived at home with Ma and Pa. But Pa put Frank out of the house when he brought Ann home. Ma and Pa were good Catholics who went to Greenfield Center Catholic Church and Sokol Hall. Frank rented George White's little house at the foot of Spruce Mountain Fire Tower road and set Ann up in housekeeping. He'd come home to her Saturday night, return early Monday morn. He worked on the house, later they bought it.

All gossip you say? I'm leading up to my story—

Joe agreed to cut some logs for Bill Coleman who owned a farm and a woodlot next to mine. In payment, Bill deeded Joe an acre lot on the fire tower road, near Frank and Ann. Joe also swapped work around for lumber, roll roofing, a window and a door and put up a small camp, near a spring. Then he brought young Olga there for their home. That led to Frank and Ann and Joe and Olga getting wed by the priest at Greenfield Center.

Ann, reformed, got a job in the shirt factory in Corinth, walking to South Corinth for her ride. Olga also reformed (we hoped) became a housewife. She also

13

became a midwife, a granny woman for local country folk. She'd learned from her mother in Europe. Besides being a granny woman she was into witchery and healing with roots and herbs.

We were fourteen miles or so to Saratoga, six miles or so to Corinth and Doctor Johnson. But sometimes Doc was on a drunk, a toot or a bender as it was called, and was not available if you got to Corinth by automobile or horse and wagon. There was talk of two nurses starting a hospital which they did later and then Doctor Snyder came to Corinth. But back then Doc Johnson was it.

So Olga and her doin's was welcome. She worked up a little trade in treating illness and healing wounds and injuries. Added to that, she began to tell fortunes with cards, teas, palm readings and going into a trance or spell. I wondered if she was a gypsy? She'd cast demons from your body, sacrifice roosters and cast spells by casting the feathers. She claimed healing agents were in your own body and she used them to help you. She also employed what seemed magical means to stop worry, fear, hate, jealousy, cure wounds and sores, headaches. Joe was right proud of his Olga. She made cash money, was given chickens, eggs, canned goods, a goat to provide milk and I don't know what all.

My brother Harry was now living at my farm. Had a potato crop in, a large garden, two cows, chickens, and some sheep. I was working in the lumber woods for cash money. Olga walked to our house to buy a few of the fleeces of wool Harry had hung in the barn. (Harry's wife had died; my Mom and Pop had his two children down on Long Island. Harry had been gassed in Europe in WWI.) Olga looked at the fleeces, then at Harry's hand. She studied the fingernails on one hand, stroked that hand, looked into his eyes. "Mister B," she said, "You are very sick man. You need help. I can no give."

14

Just then a neighbor boy on a bike came along the road. Olga sent him down the road for Jim Flynn. He and I were the only ones for miles around that had a car. A few folk had horse and wagons, many folks walked. Of course my car was parked on the mountain near my work. Jim Flynn drove to the farm and Olga told him to take Harry at once to Saratoga Hospital. Olga had earned respect from some folk, Jim among them. Jim drove to Saratoga. On the way, Harry had a blood flow from the mouth. Jim went home and got Guido Frye to ride his horse up the mountain to where I was working near Black Pond. Jim and I went to Saratoga hospital. Harry had been sedated. Doctor told me that he learned from Harry that he was a vet from WWI. Doc had already phoned the vet hospital for admission for Harry. Next day, Jim and I took Harry to the vet hospital at Crown Point.

How had Olga known that Harry was seriously ill?

With Harry in the hospital, I came down off the mountain and lived at my farm, which I very seldom did. I cut firewood for the coming winter and also cut some to sell. Now and then, Jim and I went to see Harry at vet hospital. After a couple of months we were able to bring him home. In the meantime, Joe and Olga were having trouble. She was younger than Joe, and began having an affair with a married man, whose name I won't repeat here.

The man's wife heard about it. Although she'd had Olga attend her for her last birth— a worrisome time with a breech birth—it got her blood up. She went to see Olga. There was an awful fight with blood spilled. Olga was said to have told the woman that fire would burn her house down.

Well, two nights later, that woman's house in Greenfield Township—next to the one room Brackett Corner School—was struck by lightning and burned to the ground. The family moved into a chicken coop and the

15

wife had the state police arrest Olga for assault, battery, slanderous talk, husband-stealing and arson.

Court held was in the back room of the candy store of Justice of Peace Warren (Jumbo) Saunders. I liked the folks whose house had burned, but I felt I owed Olga on account of my brother Harry. So I was a character witness for Olga. Several other people were there, but not in favor of Olga. Guido's wife Mary accused Olga of causing her miscarriage. Another lady said Olga caused her two cows to go dry and lamed the bay mare. Missus Donovan said Olga put a spell on her, made her real ill. She also accused Olga of being out behind the barn with hubby Ken. (They sold out and moved after the trial).

There were several other charges of witchcraft and another burning, a barn in that case. But the most sensational of all was when Joe appeared. Bill Coleman brought him up to Corinth by horse and wagon. I had given Olga a ride in my car. Joe told the J.P. that his wife Olga had bewitched him and carried on with other men. He didn't want her around any more.

Jumbo told Joe he'd have to get a lawyer and go to county court. He said most of the charges against Olga was what he called, "Old Women's Talk." He did not believe enough of anything was proven. Whether the charges against Olga were true or not he could see trouble coming and things were just going to get worse. Jumbo told Olga that she had better move out of the Township of Corinth, until she got things straightened out in county court. So Olga moved out.

A little while after that I stopped in the North Greenfield store for some Chevalte wurst which they sold and I liked. Lo and behold, there was Olga, just as pretty and pleasant as ever. She told me she was living with a Polish family nearby. Olga said she was doing birthin', healing, fortunes and casting spells. However, she'd be leaving soon. She had an offer to go down near

16

Saratoga Lake to work for a rich lady who wanted her fortune told every day. And that was the last I heard from Olga.

Just about the time that Olga left, Joe was found dead on the way to his camp from his spring. The bucket was on the ground, tipped over. It was as if the water ran from the container at the same time the life slipped from the body of Joe, the woodchopper.

THE WITCH OF
BRIMSTONE HILL

The name Brimstone Hill was put upon the hill and house on top of it, because an old granny lady and herb doctor who lived there told how she had been visited by a big shiny thing that came out of the sky and shot lights and smoke that smelled like brimstone or sulphur from the Pits of Hell. It had some kind of people in it. She said she chased it away by showing a cross to the critters.

The granny lady, like many others of her kind, lived alone. And while folks was kind of scared of her, they called upon her to come to house or cabin when there was gonna be a birthin', or broke bone, sickness or such like. It was miles and miles to a doctor by horse and wagon.

Granny never used coal oil or lamps at home. Always candles she made of beeswax, tallow and herbs. She had a tin candle mold and made for herself and sold some to back country folk who called 'em tapers. They believed a lit taper at night kept summer bugs away, and its smell at any time warded off evil and owls and bats. Night creatures. At the same time the wonderful tapers brought good fortunes to a dwelling.

Granny, if she was indeed a witch, was a good witch, a white Wwitch who had no black or evil traits. That is most folks considered her so. With her herbs and candles and chants she could talk evil spirits away from a home or family. If you wanted to cleanse your home of the evil beings that caused troubles and fights in families then you'd go get Brimstone Granny.

If man and wife were fighting, Granny used honey, cinnamon and lavender flowers for them to drink. If a man was out of work, he could go see Granny. She'd give him a mixture of raw egg in goat's milk with some kind of herbs stirred in. Then she'd tell him where to find work at some lumber camp, saw mill, or hardwood handle factory. Dad-burn many a feller did get work and then go back to Granny and cross her palm with silver, as a "Thank you, Ma'am."

She sold dried herbs and made up potions and amulets to wear around the neck. Once they wanted Granny to cure a victim bit by a timber rattler.

"No sir," she says. "A sarpint is pure poison. The work of Satan. Ain't no herb, not even snakeweed, to cure a rattler. Get the poor feller to a doctor at once. Don't spare the horse. Git goin'!"

She used to tell people that whoever dressed an infant the first time should always use care to place the child's right arm in the sleeve first, to assure that the child grew up right-handed. The first dress put on a child should be new. An old one would cause it to grow up a sloppy person. Place a horseshoe with nails in it in a child's crib or cradle. It leads to good health. Keep the nails away from the baby. If a baby seemed to have spells, put it three times through a horse collar, taken from a horse when it is still warm. What's more, tickling a child before it is a year old could cause it to stammer.

Granny had one bad case. The man mistrusted his wife. Then she gave birth to twins that Granny said were beautiful and healthy. The man was still suspicious of his wife and kept carrying on about her. He said he knew one of them was his'n. But the other "Pup" was a stranger. He'd have none of it, despite his wife's pleas. He even said he'd drown it in the river, like any unwanted pup.

Granny knew a woman upriver who'd lost a new-

19

born baby. She sent the unwanted child upriver and the woman was so pleased and happy and she took it, wet nursed it and raised it as her own and her husband was pleased. The person that told me this story said the twins, boys, grew up apart and still looked and acted like one another.

Granny said if a sick person got bedsores the thing to do was lay an axe under the bed and wash the sores twice a day and turn the sick person over.

Granny got old, real old. Died nice and peaceable in her own bed. They got that there barber man from down to Conklinville to build her a nice pine box out of smooth lumber for her to go in.

The preacher said Granny was a good lady and gave her a service and let her be buried in his church yard. I feel good to be able to tell a good story of Granny. God Rest Her Soul!

Many witch women died a rough death I was told.

WHEN YOU LOSE A CHILD

The witch lady was called to the house at Big Tree because she was also a granny woman, versed in the healing with herbs, roots and prayers. She gave teas to drink and applied pads and poultices for hurts, injuries and sickness.

The woman of the house at Big Tree had stabbed her little girl and then herself. She'd done it because she wanted them both to join her little boy in Heaven. The boy had drowned the week before in the river. The mother and little girl had been found bleeding, by a neighbor who came to buy some eggs. It was she who ran to the witch for help.

The witch-granny woman treated both the injured. She also sent the neighbor lady to fetch the Town Constable. The Constable placed the woman under arrest and escorted the mother and daughter down to the hospital at Saratoga Springs, where both were given additional treatment. Both lived. The mother was placed in County Jail at Ballston Spa.

The witch explained to people that the death of any person, especially a child is a shock to anyone. The mother could not deal with the sudden death of her little boy. The husband was away, working in the lumber woods up north. The woman could not handle the loss alone. If she had kept the boy at home that day he would not have drowned.

"When you lose a parent, you lose your past," said the witch. "When you lose a child," she continued, "You lose your future!"

MADE A PACT
WITH A WITCH

We stood looking at a rundown farm in the woods. There was an old grey house long neglected, badly in need of paint and repairs. Its doors were hanging, its windows broken, the yard grown up with tall grass and weeds. Next to it was a barn with a swayback roof and double wide doors flat on the ground, grass and weeds growing through all the cracks. There was also a shed, half torn down. What was left of it was newer, better lumber than house or barn.

Barn swallows, zipping around overhead with their cheerful cries of tweet-tweet-tweet, were the only signs of life in the area. The year was 19 and 28. This house had belonged to a lady who came to be feared and shunned by the local folks, because she made a pact with a witch.

Wayne Cosden and his wife Lisa had been pretty well-to-do before his death. Wayne had loaned out money to folks in the valley, charging interest and demanding a share of the crops or some of the hogs or cattle as return on the loan. It was a long way to a bank in those horse and wagon days and took many hours of travel. Furthermore, to obtain a bank loan a feller had to just about prove he didn't need a loan in order to get one.

So Wayne did business in his own hard-hearted way. He kept most of his figures of outstanding debts in his head. He could hardly write his own name, but was a very shrewd man and rose above his lack of schooling. When Wayne died his wife did not know who owed her what. People thought this was a good time to get even with that old skinflint Wayne. They did not worry about the widow nor did they tell Lisa how much they owed her. They made no payments. Lisa began to feel hard times. She knew that money was out there and should be coming to her. She began to cast about for some way to solve her problems.

A lady name of Karen Coker lived upriver at Dead Horse Eddy, heard that a Mister K was bragging that he had made an agreement with Wayne Cosden and he was not going to pay the widow, not a dollar on the debt. So Karen Coker, who was a Witch-Woman took it upon herself to visit Lisa Cosden. Over a cup of tea Karen told Lisa that she knew Mister K could pay the debt in full. For a fee to be paid by Lisa, Karen would see that the debt was paid. This was wonderful news to the poor widow and she made a pact with the Witch-Lady.

The debt was on the original agreement that the loan was to be repaid in full. Wayne Cosden was also supposed to have gotten a share of the crop of corn to sell as his own or put-it-by to feed his own stock in winter. The crib of corn was in the farmyard of Mister K. The door of the crib was locked. The date of the payment was to have been on the day of the full moon. The witch Karen had heard of this.

The day of the due payment came and the farmer Mister K paid nothing to the widow. That night, all the corn disappeared from the locked crib. The farmer was very angry the next morn and accused some of his neighbors of stealing his corn. They denied any knowledge of it. Then a boy came in the Croweville store, from the river. He heard the talk and he said that he had just seen an ear of corn on the ground at the lane going into the widow's place.

Mister K high tailed it over to see the widow. There he found the two women and a large pile of corn on the barn floor. He demanded his corn. Karen, the Witch, told him if he did not pay his debt to the widow, plus a share of the corn, it would disappear and he would never see it again. Also, she told him that he should go home and say his prayers as dire things could happen to him.

This scared Mister K. He raced his horse to the village and to his home. He returned to the two ladies, paid his debt in cash money and also agreed on how many bushels of corn the widow could keep and sell. Mister K was told to return home. The next morning, there was corn in his corn crib and the door locked.

This story began to worry other men who were in debt to the widow, through having owed her husband. The pact between Lisa and Karen continued. Horses, cows, sheep, and pigs began to disappear. Several men in the valley came down sick. Wives got after husbands to pay debts. This caused family arguments.

The preacher, a part-time minister, and rest of the time farmer, denounced the two women for using witchery and said they were in cahoots with the Devil. Then it turned out the preacher owed the widow. He had borrowed money from Wayne to buy a pregnant sow and he was also supposed to give Wayne the money and two shoats.

Pretty soon the widow began to receive money, livestock, shares of corn and wheat. The two women did all right for themselves and things quieted down in that section of the Valley.

Time passed. Then the word was put out that there would be a dam built on the river "Sacandog" as the Indians called it. Every one would have to sell their property for the reservoir project and either move their buildings or leave them to be torn down and burned. The state only wanted the land! The two women, Karen and Lisa, were among the very first to sell their lands in the year 19 and 25 to the Hudson River Regulating District. They moved, leaving their homes.

Karen Coker was one witch-lady who did not meet a tragic end to her life, as happened to many women who practiced Witchcraft and were in league with The Devil. The old house of the Widow Cosden was a lonely place when Lou and I saw it and began to demolish it as part of our job.

There were many stories told under the wood-shingled roof and I have just shared one with you—another story of the Sacandaga.

THE HOUSE OF
DOOM AT BIG HELL

It was an old house and I mean old. Never painted, the wood boards had turned grey—a dismal grey. It did not shine as a grey color in sunlight, but was a dead grey. On the rear of the building it was greenish black halfway up to the roof like the moss that forms on many tree trunks on the side not exposed to the sunlight. The windows also were gloomy, most glass panes either broken out or removed by someone who had wanted or needed the glass.

The broken windows made the house sort of gape at me, like a cut-out pumpkin at Jack o' Lantern time. Lou said, "Makes the old house look toothless with just a few snags showing like old Granpaw Mosher."

The bricks in the central chimney were tumbled down, on the ground, with one still on the slanty roof. Could have been a target for hunters, or just old age working on it.

That house at "Big Hell" had been empty for years. We stepped up on the shaky porch and entered a door-less room. There were some pieces of furniture there, a broken bed, broken leg table, chairs, and old wood and a canvas army cot. Papers, clothes, and old shoes were scattered around the floor. An old shoe, is a sad, dismal sight, I think.

Then we went in a couple more rooms, just junk, trash there. Finally we came to the back room. This was the room we wanted to see—to see if what we had heard would be there and if it was really what it was said to be.

It was! A coffin set on some sort of a little metal rack. We said something like "Holy Cow! I don't believe it" and "It sure enough is a coffin!"

We stepped over to it. The lid was on the floor, with what were axe marks in it. The coffin, it really was a casket, had been bought in town and was not just a pine box made of unpainted lumber, showed age and abuse. The handles had been removed. The lining in it was faded, torn and we could see that it had been a porcupine nest and smelled like it. This was the coffin we had wanted to see. So, some of the stories could be true. It was said that this old house had belonged to an old witch. She in turn had been the daughter of a witch, giving the house the name, "The House of Doom" at "Big Hell Farm."

Many were the stories that Lou, my working partner and friend, and I had heard about this place in the Valley. We were working at that time on the demolition crew, called "The Barn Busters" on the project of construction of the first Sacandaga Dam.

Before we started to tear down the house, we were required to examine the barn and sheds and make sure no one was asleep or hiding in the old buildings to avoid accidents. But this place in particular we sure wanted to look over.

The old lady that had lived there had been known as a witch woman. At the moment one of the stories we were most interested in was the one about her husband Rick, who had drowned in the river. The next day, a boy from a nearby farm had brought the widow a young raven that he had taken from a nest in some rocks on the mountain up back. He knew the woman Hattie was very fond of birds and animals and she gave him some homemade cookies for bringing the bird to her.

Hattie believed in many bizarre things and when she heard the young bird cry, to her it was the hoarse voice of her departed husband. Rick had been reincarnated in this young raven. To her mind this was logic, as she saw it. She had lost her husband and the very next morning the raven that sounded like Rick was brought to her. This was the new Rick!

She raised it as though it were a child, talking to it all the time. In time the raven began to answer her. Repeating her words, the speech of the bird improved. Now she was sure the voice was that of her lost husband reincarnated in the raven. She even gave the husband's name to the bird and from then on it was "Rick the Raven". Hattie swore the bird acted like the dead man and possessed the man's knowledge and memories.

Hattie told the boy's mother who lived about a mile upriver that "her husband," meaning the raven, had told her she should purchase a casket and set it up in the back room for him to rest in. The body of Rick was never found in the river and therefore there had been no burial. So Hattie paid the neighbor lady and her husband to drive her, in their horse and wagon to far off Glens Falls to purchase a casket and bring it home. The raven often slept in the coffin and Hattie believed it was her dead husband at rest.

Widow Hattie was a granny lady, always had been. She attended birthin's as a midwife, treated ailments with herbs and roots and such like. For a donation she would place a curse on animal or human and sold amulets, talismans and good luck charms and stones, told fortunes and was believed to be steeped in mystery and magic. She also sold locally made hooch to lumberjacks, farm hands and rivermen who came to her place.

One stormy night a logger was drinking at her place. He asked to be allowed to sleep in and not walk the wet, muddy road in the pouring rain and darkness. He offered to pay to sleep anywhere in a dry place. He said later that the raven told the lady "Let him sleep! Let him sleep."

She offered him the casket to sleep in. The half-drunk feller took the offer as a joke and slept in the bizarre resting place. In the morn he awoke refreshed and with a wonderful story of a dream. This story he told up and down the river. And, by-Gee, he was believed and soon other men were asking to be able to pay a fee even on a clear night, so they could sleep in the casket. Sort of strange early-day bed and breakfast.

It was believed that if you slept in the coffin, your soul was sent out on a journey of death. That is, you saw death in one form or another. Then you were re-called to their own body in the magic casket and there-after you never feared death again.

No doubt Hattie used herbs in her drink and food that produced hallucinating dreams and sleep. A pinch of jimson weed or poke and two pinches or so can put a feller into eternal dreamland. It was believed that a couple of bodies in the river came from the House of Doom, but never proved.

There were several stories of men being close to death in accidents in sawmills and in the lumber woods who escaped death. One man was even shot and did not die. All claimed to have slept in the coffin. The house with the raven became very popular. Of course, those stories made Hattie's place a lure to a certain ele-ment of males. Others, especially women, looked down upon her and her friends.

Then one day Hattie was at the river washing clothes. The raven was with her picking up bright peb-bles and carrying them to where she was. Suddenly a large bird flew over and swooped down to attack the raven. The farm boy was fishing nearby and saw it all—he grew up and later years, I heard the whole story from him, much as I've been telling it.

The raven screamed "Help! Help!" and Hattie ran to help. The big bird seized Rick the Raven and Hattie ran out deeper and deeper into the water and was swept away as Rick was carried across the river, never to be seen again. The boy ran home for help but when folks returned with him, Hattie was gone. Her body was recovered next day and was buried in the Church yard at Huntsville. I was told a plain pine box was used. No one wanted to get the coffin from the house.

Neither Hattie or Rick the Raven ever were reincarnated, leastwise never that I was told. The house and coffin were empty for years, until our foreman told us to tear it down and pile the remains for the crew of Barn Burners who came along to complete the job. Remember, there was smoke in the valley for two years as the project work was done. Then the flood waters in the year 19 and 30 covered everything except the memories of a few of us old timers who can remember the story of the House of Doom at Big Hell Farm and what it and the coffin looked like.

BONE DROP CAVE

Avery Hunt claimed to be from a long line of Hunts that went back, way back to about the year 18 and 36. A feller back then name of Amos Hunt had a tavern near the river. The area came to be known as Huntsville, later called Croweville, then West Day.

Well, Avery told me of an old Granny Woman who was also a witch. Among other things, she used to send folks that came to her, and wanted to have a wish come true, up on the mountain. After that, they gave her an offering of coins, or a chicken, or eggs or even hog fat.

The wishers were to follow an old blazed trail on the mountain to an opening in the ground, among some rocks. That place was later known locally as "Bone Drop Cave". The witch told them to carry an animal bone to the place. There they were to place the bone on the ground close to the hole, repeat some sort of prayer she'd given them, turn around three times, make the wish out loud to the spirits of the forest, then nudge the bone into the hole with the left foot. The hole was believed to be a deep, bottomless pit. It was also said that there was a wide, circle, made of piled stones around Bone Drop Cave. Whether witches had made the big circle of stones, or early Indians for some sort of ceremony was not known.

So, one Sunday when we did not have to work on the project, Avery and I took lunches and went up on the mountain. We searched all day for that ring of piled up stones and the cave. We found neither, but had a pleasant day in the forest hunting for the old, old story.

"GO TELL IT TO THE BEES"

That was an old saying and belief that came to the new country and the valley from Europe.

Many farms and estates in old Britain and France kept hives of bees to make their fruit trees and crops more productive and, of course, for the honey produced by the bees. Bees have been domesticated by man for hundreds, even thousands of years. Honey bees are friendly with the beekeeper who cares for them and their hives. It's said they even have an uncanny affection for the bee-person. When a beekeeper dies, the bees appear very upset and all fly up to circle and circle and circle in the air around their hives. Sometimes even fly to the house of the deceased and cluster around the doors and windows.

This was observed, many, many years ago in Europe. So it became the custom when the beekeeper died to have some one go out to the hives of bees and call out: "The Master is dead! The Master is Dead!" Then, it was claimed, the bees settled down. I was told that in one section of Britain, it was the custom for some member of the family to go to the hives and drape a piece of black cloth on each hive. The same thing was done on the front door of the home of the dead person. I'll add that when I was a boy and there was a death in our house we had a big black bow with streamers attached to our front door. And the members of the family each wore a black arm band on their coat. There used to be a period of mourning.

If the custom was not carried out to tell the bees of a death, you perhaps are wondering, then what happened

with the bees? That is what I am leading up to, in my own way.

Just when I entered the U.S. Army Air Corps in the year 19 and 42—for the duration as my papers read—I thought that I had found the girl of my dreams. So, I purchased a house on Luzerne Bay where the Sacandaga River joins the North River to form the Hudson River—as the local people say. (Actually the Hudson River rises deep in the 'Dacks in Mount Marcy country, at a lovely place called "Lake Tear of the Clouds"—a place as lovely as the name.)

Anyway, I rented out that house till the war was over. The man I purchased the house from was originally a French-Canadian, who had come south and settled in the Sacandaga Valley and then had to sell his lands there to the state for the dam to be built. A displaced person, he purchased the house on Luzerne Bay and went to work in the paper mill at Corinth-Palmer Falls. The man's name was Ami Daniels. He told me that when he lived in the Valley he kept bees on his farm. He knew of the custom of telling the bees on the death of the beekeeper. But most folks said it was just superstition. A silly, old belief.

Then a man died who kept bees near Osborn Bridge. A grave was dug in the church yard and the man was to be buried that day. When the pine box with the body was carried from the house, the bees became excited and flew around the pall bearers and the wagon the coffin was placed in. The horse and people became very upset, but they made it to the burial ground. But the bees had followed the wagon and they swarmed in a mass at the top of the open grave. People were too scared to continue with the funeral. Some people even left the grave yard because of the many bees.

Then someone thought they should send for Ami Daniels the Beeman. So a man rode a horse to get Ami. He hitched his horse and wagon, loaded on some hives and drove to the graveyard. When Ami got there he talked to the bees as if they were little people, got the Queen and put her in a hive and the bees swarmed around his wagon. When they settled down, Ami drove off with the bees to his own little farm and added the bees to those he had. The man was buried in his grave and things went smoothly. The widow sent word to Ami that he was to keep the bees.

Ami told me of another beekeeper near Beecher's Hollow who died. His people didn't tell the bees of his death. The bees gathered and followed the funeral to the Buryin' Ground and actually swarmed in a mass on the pine coffin as it was lifted from the wagon. Again Ami Daniels was sent for to calm the bees and get them to go in the hives he provided. Only then was the funeral completed.

Ami said he hated to give up farming and beekeeping when he had to sell out to the project. He took his bees, with hives to the edge of the forest and left them to go wild because they were little friends to him and he hated to sell them. And he spoke to those bees and said, "Good Bye!"

Honeybees seem to have minds of their own!

WHY SEND FOR A
GRANNY WOMAN?

Me believe in witchcraft? Heck. I'm sort of the result of it in a way.

In the Valley, more often than not, a woman about to give birth would not have a doctor even if one were within reach in the days of travel by horse. She would send someone to fetch the local Granny Woman, who was very capable as a midwife at a birthin', even though she might be considered a local witch.

Strange? No. For the custom of the times, I guess it could be called the culture of the times, forbade a woman to undress before a man. So the average woman would not undress before a male doctor. Only her husband was to see her disrobed. And there were no women doctors far out in country towns. In big cities perhaps? Not only was an average woman excessively shy and not having faith in a doctor then. She would have been embarrassed, even humiliated.

I was the last child of seven to be borne by my mother. The family lived in a small town. There was a doctor in town, some miles away, but within reach there was a hospital. However, it was more or less believed then, when I was born over 85 years ago, that hospitals were places to go to die. Or perhaps have an arm or leg cut off, if need be.

To some folks to have a baby in a hospital then, meant the baby was unprotected against evil spirits. At home there was only love. A home born baby was more protected.

So, my mother's seven children were all born at

home. The local doctor was there because my parents were not too old-fashioned. I remember being told years later that one of my sisters and the brother. just a year older than me, were fifteen ($15.00) dollar babies. I was a twenty five ($25.00) dollar baby. That was the doctor's fee.

In later years, up in the valley, I learned that oft times the granny lady would place a Bible at the head of the birthin' bed and a pair of shears, and a measuring rule at the other end of the bed.

Strange? No. Let me explain, the belief as it was explained to me by an old granny woman who was also a witch. Why she even had a pet owl. The Bible, measuring rule and shears were useful in this way: if an evil spirit should enter the room and see those three witch-placed objects, the evil force would at once be slowed down by the Bible. Then the spirit could be measured and cut up into pieces. So, to protect itself, the spirit would flee the room and the house.

Now, that kind of needful protection could not be had at a hospital or a doctor's office. For there were strangers there in a strange place who could place or cast the "evil eye" on the child, mother, or both.

If a person, man or woman got stomach pains, that could be from an "evil eye". Or if they had reason to worry about their own deeds, then it could be believed the pains were punishment from God. If that were the belief, no doctor could be of help. "Please send for the granny woman," folks would say—the witch in other words. Her herbs, potions and mumblings would then probably cure the "belly-ache." Unfortunately if it was a busted "pendix", and the sufferer died, then that was "God's Will."

So belief and custom were the order of the day, helped as well by many, many miles of travel over bad roads to remote places.

A belief in witchcraft was found in some parts of the

valley. Brought from the Old World across the sea. Ancient beliefs, superstitions and legends, different religions from different folk and they found that the Native Americans the Indians, had their own medicine men, Shamen, and witch doctors and Powwow doctors.

So, if a person practiced the Black Art, believed in Satan and ghosts and strange creatures, that was often left up to them. As long as they left you alone. The early years of the Salem Witch Trials having passed. A person did not have to serve an apprenticeship, or go to a witch school or graduate from a school for witch doctors. It seemed if they were, they were. Who cared? Except to gossip?

A granny woman would be called to a home for a birthin' or to heal the sick with herbs, poultices and the use of strange words. Even set a broken bone. There always seemed to be enough call or business if I may put it that way. Truth was truth and who knew what. A person, usually a woman, could be found to have the reputation as a witch. They were not guilty unless so charged and proven of any overt acts of witchcraft.

Can superstition be a peril? Was or is there such as a Wisdom Stone, a magic stone used for fortunes, even to tell of death or point the hand of death? Can a witch truly ride a person at night, or was it a bad dream?

Did the triangular shape cut into the lintels of doors in the house and barn at Misery Hill bring illness and death to beasts in the barn and humans in the house on the hill? Or was it just a queer belief and did the happenings on Misery Hill just happen by chance?

What about the farm house I visited that day when the butter was hard to churn? Then the lady tried without success to boil milk on the stove to cook something. Suddenly she grabbed a sharp, long handle fork and she plainly said to the pot of milk as she jabbed the milk in it, "Get out! Get out! And stay away you imp of Satan!" A believer, she was sure the pot and its contents were bewitched.

She told me that the "night beings", the phosphorescent lites in the damp fields and woodlands that appear and disappear and appear again are unhappy spirits. Some folks called them "jack o' lanterns," those strange lites. I guess the name through the years has come to be used on Halloween night?

When I worked on the project I had many jobs. On the demolition crew(we were called the Barn Busters) I found a pile of dusty old books in an old empty house on Dead Mule Road, where I was told a Dutchman or German feller had lived. Nobody else wanted any so I took the whole pile. Later I sold most at what seemed a good price then.

But one book I kept for a while. It was, "Pow-wow, or the Long Lost Friend." I later sold that at a good price. It was sort of a witch guide of what to do. Most of it was prayers and incantations as I recall.

THE CAT'S PAW

Thoughrold Tyndall ran a sawmill at Fox Haven. He was called a tightwad. He paid fair wages to his help, but he wouldn't pay unless you stayed a month. A couple men stayed on the job, but most quit in a couple weeks. That gave Thoughrold their work for free. Those that quit went to the village of Beecher's Hollow and said that Thoughrold must be in league with the Devil. Because after they'd been there a little while a witch would come at them in the night and scare them out of the bunk in the shanty, warning them that they must leave. So they got out.

Ricky Redman was working with me on the dam. He told me the stuff I've just told you. His father's brother needed work. He'd heard of the doin's at Fox Haven Mill but he decided a job was a job. Witch or no witch. So he took the job. It later turned out he stayed on the job several years. He became head sawyer. It came about in this way, as Ricky told it.

When his uncle got the job, he was given a shack to live in. The witch came to his shack after a few nights. She was a scary-looking person. She hissed at him and told him to be gone or the Devil would get his soul.

But Ricky's uncle, he didn't scare. He was a church-going man and a good Christian. He had a small Bible tucked in his pack sack. The next night, he knew the moon would shine bright, so he put the Bible on a block of wood next his bunk. That moonlit night the witch came again into the shack, probably through the open window. She hissed and growled at him and made motions with her hands as if she'd scratch his eyes out.

41

Real quick-like, Ricky's uncle grabbed his little Bible and held it up toward the face of the witch. She backed off and the next thing he knew she was gone and there was a big black cat there trying to claw at him and hissing something awful.

Uncle had been born over near to Munsonville at the edge of the Big Vly. He'd heard tell of witches and demons turning into animals. So he figured the witch was still there in the form of that nasty fearsome black cat. He grabbed his razor sharp double bit axe and swung at the cat as if he were to cut a beech tree down. Just then the cat made a lunge with a front paw at him. The axe clipped that paw and cut it clean off. The cat yowled and made a three-legged jump out the window, leaving bloody marks on the sill.

Uncle tied a rawhide thong around the cat's paw and hung it on a nail in the wall. After a bit he went back to sleep. In the morning when he awoke he thought he'd gone through a bad dream. But then, as he sat up in his bunk and reached for his shoes, he saw the Bible and the blood on the rough wood floor. Raising his eyes he saw the cat's paw hanging from the nail on the wall.

He made a fire in the wood stove and boiled some coffee and ate some cold corn dodgers with it. For tight-fisted Thoughrold Tyndall did supply his men with some scant rations. Then Uncle went to work at the sawmill, wearing the severed cat paw on the thong looped around his neck. The other couple fellas working saw it but said nothing, like as if they might know something.

After a couple of hours the boss man Mister Tyndall drove up to the mill with a team and wagon to get a load of lumber to deliver.

He saw the cat's paw on the thong around Uncle's neck, called him aside, gave him his pay and told him that he could stay at the mill.

Uncle heard the next day that the old aunt of

Thoughrold Tyndall had been found downriver, dead. One of her hands was missing. It was figured that she'd fell in the river and that a big snapping turtle or some other critter had bit the hand off.

Uncle kept the dried cat's paw for years. Ricky Redman said he'd seen the cat's paw when he was a little boy at the turn of the century.

THE EMPTY GRAVES

Let me tell you a strange true story about a buryin' ground. You see when they built that there dam at Conklingville on the Sacandaga, there was a whole passel of folks that had to move outta the valley. Before the project workers could build the dam and power house, they had to clear the whole valley. The work crews had to cut miles of trees and brush and burn 'em. They had to demolish all houses, shacks, barns, stores, churches, mills and such and burn the lumber. At the church yards and private buryin' grounds, they had to dig up the buried remains of a many folks long gone and then transplant 'em to other places above where the high water line would come.

Well, my story has to do with a little church way out in the boondocks. The Gospel House on Windswept Hill, I'll call it, because it might upset and stir up some livin' folks if they heard the name of that meetin' house their ancestors went to. A gang of men was workin' in what we called the "Bone Yard Gang." Diggin' up the old graves, you understand.

So they came to the little Gospel House, all empty now. Alongside it was a buryin' ground with a little picket fence around it and what were called grave markers inside. The two fellers that could write, they got busy and made up a sort of map of the grave spots and headstones and gave each one a number. They got their paper work done and then the pick and shovel boys went to work diggin' up the first couple of graves. Pretty soon, though, they yelled real loud for the foreman, the boss man of the crew.

44

When he got there they showed him that in those first couple of graves there was nary hide, nor hair nor a single bone. That caused a commotion. The two map makers wrote down words on a paper. Well, that happened in every grave they dug up until noonin'. Then they all sat around a campfire eating their grub and, of course, talking and wonderin' what was wrong with these graves, since they ain't found nary a bone.

Just then an old man come along. He told his name and said he lived up on the mountain nearby. When he saw the smoke of their campfire he come to see how they was doin'. They gave him a sangwich or two and some coffee and told him about the mystery of where the bones had done went.

That old mountain man laughed, slapped his thigh in glee and told them he knew this was sure gonna happen when he heard there was to be a diggin' up of all the graves in the valley and movin' of the bones.

"Years ago," he said, "an old settler gave a preacher man a piece of his land, this piece right here. If the preacher would stay and build up a congregation, the old man would have a small church built, so his grand-kids could attend. The preacher agreed to stay and so the Gospel House and a house for the preacher were built.

People came from miles around to hear ol' fashioned "Fire and Brimstone" and "Drive the Devil from your lives and away from your souls." People liked it. But Old Nick, he didn't like it. Some say his devilish imps told him about the goings on up at Windswept Hill.

So, the Devil, he made Windswept Hill almost as hot as Hell, with real hot winds, instead of the cool winds the folk were used to. Folks didn't like it, but they didn't want to move. There was work in a saw mill, a feldspar mine and logs to be cut in the woods. So they stayed. But, like anywhere else, now and then some one would get killed in the loggin' woods by a falling tree

45

or in the mine by a fallin' rock or just get sick and die. Being as how Old Nick was the Devil, when that happened, he sent a real hot wind and the dead person just dried up and blew away.

The preacher man, he saw that he was up against a bitter foe. But he was not to be outdone. Whenever a death occurred, even though the body had dried up and blew away, the preacher still held a service, saying prayers to save the soul, even though there was no body to be buried. The folks went along with that and planted a grave marker for every person who died and was taken by the Devil Wind.

"And that was why," said the Old Mountain Man, "There are no bones to be found by diggin. 'Cause there never was no bodies planted in the earth."

The grave markers were moved sure enough by the Bone Yard Gang. They never heard what the map makers or the boss man reported to the higher-up people in Albany. But there were sure enough empty graves at the Gospel House Buryin' Ground.

You can use me for bear bait if I ain't told you the true of it, as I heard it.

AUNT MILLIE AND THE DISAPPEARANCES

Aunt Millie, as everyone called her, lived in the valley in a wood frame house on a few acres in the area called West Day. By some folk she was believed to be a witch. She was believed to have caused the death or disappearance of two men. That's correct. Just disappeared. Gone!

Aunt Millie, I'll not mention her last name, 'cause relatives might still be living, was a widow lady. Her husband had been killed by a tree he was felling in the woods. The tree got hung up in standing trees, he tried to get it down. We used to call such a cut tree a "Widow Maker." A tree that went part way down and fell into and bowed over other trees was called a "Fool Killer." Those bowed trees had to be cut in a certain way for safety.

Aunt Millie knew the dam was to be put in the river and flood the lands, hers included. But Millie, like many others, did not want to leave her home. Millie had some goats for milk and cheese. Hogs for meat and lard. Chickens for eggs and stew meat. She also had a nice dog and a pet owl. Her other wants were simple, some coal oil for the lamps, Lucifers (matches), salt and flour or corn meal.

Aunt Millie was a midwife, a granny woman. She also was a sort of herb doctor and could even set some broken bones if need be. Some people considered her a witch. She was the best at a birthin', knowledgeable and experienced in any trouble that arose. In those days

47

a doctor if any was miles and miles away by horse travel or by wagon.

Millie also told fortunes for a small fee, reading the leaves from the bottom of a cup of tea. She had a deck of cards she carried in an old wool knitted sock—claimed the sock came off a dead man she found hanging from a tree. She also had a natural tourmaline crystal she'd dug up. She'd look in that semi-precious gem stone and tell a person's future. (I had three such crystals I'd dug up, later, over near Dailey Creek way. One was big as my fist. All I could ever see in it was the deep blackness and the shine of the smooth outside.) Anyway, rural folks didn't have much entertainment those days. So some folks had Millie tell their fortunes and tell what she saw.

And now the authority wanted her land. You could move your house to somewhere else or tear off boards and beams to use elsewhere. Or you could do what most folks had already done—move out, just leave house and barns empty to be torn down and burned. But you had to go.

Aunt Millie, however, said she'd seen her own future. She'd not leave her house, her place, she'd not sell and she'd not ever walk off it. Not ever! Flood waters be damned, she'd not walk off. Her stone told her so. So Aunt Millie, her stone, her owl, dog, goats and hens just stayed at the house at Black Eagle Thicket.

Feller from the state came to talk to her. She told him, "Go roll a butternut around the barn."

Then two men arrived at Millie's place. They were real official. They had proper court papers to evict her. But instead of just puttin' her furniture and stuff on the beaten ground outside her house, they'd load the stuff on the truck and take it up and across the survey line where the flood waters would stop. She had to go—Now! That's what their papers said. The rest, no one is sure about . . .

49

Some claim the two men were deputy sheriff men. Some said they were sworn-in constables. But Aunt Millie didn't go. Nor was she moved by the men with the truck. Why? Because the truck didn't move from where the two men parked it. Nor were the two men ever seen again. They had just gone, disappeared, it was discovered at day's end. The two men didn't come back and file their reports on the eviction of Millie. It was assumed they had truck trouble and were late and went straight home.

But then the wife of one man and the mother of the other got worried at the men not returning home. Late at night they told someone. It was decided a search would be made in the morning. Maybe they were walking home, got tired and slept in an empty house or barn, on some hay or straw. The next morn, early, someone drove to Aunt Millie's, still searching along the way to no avail. When they saw the truck at Millie's, all she would tell them was that the men had been there. Now they were gone.

Those two men would not leave her or her things alone, she said. In fact, two chairs had been placed in the truck and were there. Only two chairs. Nothing else. Millie said the men scoffed at her and her stone and said, "You have to go!" So she, with her stone, sent them into a space between this world and the next world.

It is said she cackled then and her eyes shone like fire. She is then reported as saying, "When those men and whoever sent them repent and allow me to stay in my own home, then and only then, shall they return at my say-so. Otherwise they are lost forever!" Millie then rubbed her crystal and started talking to it.

Searches were made for miles around the area. A newspaper called Millie a charlatan—a crazy old woman who might have somehow killed the two men. Teams of horses and plows tore up the ground. The well was probed. Down at the river, pools were searched with poles prodding and big hooks on lines. Men in boats combed the river, especially down stream. The men were missing, gone with no trace. Millie laughed and cackled. "They Gone," she'd say and cuddle her owl.

Could Millie have actually made the two men disappear? Some folk believed she could, for after all she could tell fortunes. Others claimed that was crazy talk, by people that had had to leave the valley. The house was searched, top to bottom. No secret rooms, no hollow walls, or false floors. The chimney was measured but no men, no bodies were found, not even the eviction papers the men were to have served. Of course Millie could have burned them.

So, another set of eviction papers was drawn up to be served on the little old lady. There were no legal charges against her otherwise. The days of the Salem witch Trials were long gone. And was Aunt Millie even a witch?

When another couple of men arrived at the house at Black Eagle Thicket in the valley and the men approached, with some witnesses, to hand Millie the legal papers, Millie screamed at them and reached for her stone. But one of the men, real quick-like, grabbed it first.

Millie screamed again and fell down in a faint, a fit, or a spell as some said. So Aunt Millie was carried out to a car and taken to a doctor. Aunt Millie's fortune telling came true—she never walked off her land!

That's right, she was carried off. Later she was taken from the doctor to the home of a nephew. He had been one of the witnesses and he took away her owl, dog, goats and chickens. The officials kept the mysterious black crystal. The house was at once torn down, board by board. There was no sign of the missing men. Even

51

the chimney was smashed to bits. The fire pit in the open fireplace, the hearth were all broken up.

I worked with the nephew of Millie on the construction of the first dam. The Conklingville Dam. He told me the story much as I've remembered to set it down here with pen on paper. He claimed that the two men had run off with two girls. Then he asked me if I might know a place where Aunt Millie could rent? Everything for miles around was taken up by people who had to move from the valley.

The farm I owned and rented out, as I was camping on the mountainside in the valley, sat next to a farm and empty house. The man had died, his widow gone north to live next to a sister. So we were able to get the house, a nice well and a garden spot for Aunt Millie for $10.00 a month rent. Of course there was no electric on the back roads in those days.

Millie lived there. She still attended birthing and sickness and such. Some folk still wondered about the disappearances of the two men. Now and then some officer of the law would come around to check on her. But most folks liked her.

I asked her once about the happenings in the valley. She said she didn't want to talk about it no more. Besides, they got her stone and she "couldn't do nothin' about it no more iffen she wanted to".

I asked to take her picture with owl and dog. Then she smiled said, "Sure 'nuff. I don't believe like my man used to. He was Injun, thought taken a pitcher was taken part of a person's soul. Go ahead, take a pitcher. My soul's belonged to the Devil for many a year now anyhow."

That was Aunt Millie. The last day of her life she attended the birthin' of a cute little baby girl. Then she walked home through the woods, "crosslots" we used to call it. As she stepped out of the woods she saw her house, owl and dog had all burned to the ground.

Someone had a hate for her and had torched it. Millie fell to the ground in another spell and never lived again.

That's the story of the lady I knew that some folks called a witch! Me? I thought she was a nice person and, if the Devil ain't got it, God Rest Her Soul!

PART TWO

SACANDAG

THREE RESTLESS SOULS

Joshua was a strange sort of man. That is he looked average, but he talked little, except about death and ghosts as a rule.

We were working near the village of Osborn Bridge. One day as we sat down to have our noon lunch, this feller Joshua, spoke up and said that he was the son of Sheri Gordley. The name meant nothing to me or the other guys. But Joshua had told us before that he had been born in a log cabin toward Beecher's Hollow, near what was now called Edinburgh, a cabin which would soon be torn down.

Well, nobody made a remark.

So Joshua said, "Ain't none of you gonna ask me who Sheri Gordley was?"

To get things rolling, because I always liked stories, I said, "Josh, you just now told us she was your mother. But there must be something you'd like to tell us about her. If so, I'd like to hear it."

"Well," says Joshua, "My ma is buried over there near the bridge in that little buryin' ground. I expect that Bone Yard Gang will be digging up her bones and the others buried there, about next week."

There were over twenty small graveyards moved before the waters flooded the valley. He looked around, but none of us made a remark, It got too quiet, so again I spoke up, "Gosh, Josh, it makes you feel sad, I bet."

Joshua said, "Yeah. Sad for her, but not my old man, the son of a buck, 'cause he's buried there, too. I hate the thought of him." Then he continued. "I told you before about ghosts. Right over there, sometimes folks who lived around here would see three ghosts of a night."

He slapped his thigh with the hand that did not hold a sandwich. "You all think I'm a mite tetched in the head, but I saw those ghosts too, like three small clouds of smoke above the ground."

One of the fellers said, "We believe you, Josh. But why is there three ghosts? Ain't one enough to make a story?"

"No. There was and I bet that there still is three ghosts. My pa was a tough old bull of a man. He used to go across the river to Batchlerville to see some girl. They'd both get drunk in the tavern. When he did come home he was mean and he'd beat up my Ma, Sheri. She was a Injun girl from Bald Mountain, that he married. Me, I'm half Injun. I was just a little tadpole then. Well Ma, she got to be friends with an Injun feller that come from Oak Mountain. He worked for Henry Cobb on his lumber job and in the sawmill."

He stopped to eat some, then, as we were getting ahead of him, eating while he talked. "Well my Pa found out that Ma was meetin' this Injun, at night in the buryin' ground. Makin' love among the grave stones and wood headboards. Pa came home early one night, half drunk and only me in the cabin and Ma gone. So Pa he took his rifle gun and went lookin'. He found his cheatin' wife sneakin' in the cemetery among the gleaming tombstones in the moonlight. Then Pa shot Ma, her InJun lover Tom, and himself. The good folk of the village let my aunt have the three bodies buried in the cemetery. But they was all restless souls and they started to roam the buryin' grounds on moon-lit nights. My aunt raised me. She seen the ghosts too.

"Now the state is diggin' up all the graveyards. Then the water will come and cover everything. I always felt sorry for my Ma Sheri, 'cause my pa was a bad man. A real bad man. He drove her to look for someone else. I hope her spirit will find some rest in the new place where they plant her."

It was truly a sad story. We finished our noonin' lunch in silence. It sure must have been rough on Joshua growing up after all that happening. It made me think what a lucky young lad I was.

INDIAN WELCH'S SHACK

We were sitting around a small campfire toasting our sandwiches and eating noon meal. Joshua spoke up, "A ghost is never seen without mittens. Have any of you ever seen one without mittens?"

None of us spoke up, so I guessed that none of us ever had seen a ghost without mittens. But did he really mean ghosts all wear mittens?

Josh told that it was an old saying and did not explain. Then Josh told us that over at the old Indian Settlement near Munsonville in Big Vly there was an old falling-down shack that was haunted for many long years. It seemed that an Indian living there had found a panther kitten at Devils' Crossing Marsh and carried it home in his pack basket. You could sell such critters to outsiders that came to the valley to fish for the big pike fish.

From the tracks, the mother cat must have followed Welch, the Indian, home. Nearby residents were horrified when they found the torn-up body and the disembodied head that rolled on the floor when some one found it. The body and head were buried over around Fish House in a small graveyard that was mostly used for Indians who were not Christians. That's the way things were those days.

At the cabin of Welch, where he had met an agonizing death from the female panther, candle lights would be seen in the empty shack. There were moans to be heard in the night. Screams, groans and crazy laughter.

Some folks said that the spirit of Welch, the Indian, hung over the place like a terrifying dark cloud. A disturbed spirit that had never accepted the fact that Welch was dead and buried, head and all, elsewhere. The spirit remained at the shack because that was the place of suffering. Josh said that the shack was like a house of horrors, truly a haunted place.

Joshua was asked why no one had ever burned the place down. He said that a couple of fellers told at the store that they had tried to torch the shack. But when they got near it, unseen forces and sounds had scared them away. So Indian Welch's shack stood there, lopsided, tumbling down.

The state crew burned it.

THE CRYING BABY

Mike Duffy and Ball Harris were crew members of the Demolition Crew, tearing down the houses, barns and buildings in the valley. This is the story they told.

As they stepped up on the porch of the old house they thought they heard a baby crying inside. They put their tools down and went looking for the baby. It was real late afternoon and the sky was black with clouds, like a storm was near. So it was pretty dark in the house. They searched every room, every closet, the cellar and attic. They found nothing. But every once in a while they heard the crying. It seemed to move around. They even looked up the chimney above the stone fireplace. But that was too dark to see anything.

It kept getting darker and darker and looking out the frameless windows they saw thick snow flakes coming down. So they decided they'd better call it a day and go check out at the time office a couple of miles away. That they did and went to the mess hall for supper chow. Then to the dorm where they slept. They told others about hearing the baby cry in the old house and not finding the baby. Some one told them that the old house was called Carn's Ruins and the place was known as Starvation Farm. For years, it had also been called the Haunted Farm.

The tale was that years before a girl had been arrested there for drowning her two year old boy in the well. She was supposed to have had a younger child. But it was not found, even though the house, barn and land had been searched. The girl said that she had given

62

it to a couple from up Stony Creek way, for fifty dollars. That was not proved. No one in Stony Creek had a child that matched the description.

The girl was committed to the state insane place out at Utica.

Several people tried to live in the Carn Place but always left—saying the place was haunted. The place was neglected and empty when the State and Regulating District bought all the lands in the valley for the dam project.

Well, the storm I speak of had only been a snow squall and the two men went back to work at the same old house. The sun was shining and things looked cheerful and bright. They heard no crying and decided it had probably been a kitten, like one the other men in the dormitory had suggested. It could have wandered into the old house and, being scared by them, had scampered ahead of them from room to room. But they both agreed it had sure sounded like a baby.

They began to take the house apart with wrecking bars, sledges and hammers. The old building was a plank house. In the olden days, some houses were built with the frame being covered with wide boards or planks that were nailed on vertical, running up and down tight together. Then over that boards were nailed in a horizontal position with what was called siding or ship-lap. That double layer of lumber made a house real sound and warmer in the winter and cooler in the summer. A few houses, as extra insulation, had sawdust between the inner planks and outer siding. Good beams and boards they removed the nails from and piled aside for the contractor to haul away. The rest they threw in loose piles. Those would be burned along with trees and brush cut by another crew. Then it all would be burned by the Barn Burners.

Mike and Bull found the skeleton of a human baby hidden in the walls of the attic. They notified the foreman, he told the timekeeper and he got the constable and state police. The skeleton was taken away.

Mike and Bull swore that they heard that crying baby before they ever heard the story that Carn's Ruins on Starvation Farm was haunted. We all wondered, did they really hear the crying of the lost soul of the baby? Or was it a lost kitten after all? Then the flood waters covered the site. But not the memories of some of us still alive!

THE GIRL AT RIFKIN RAPIDS

George told it to us one day at lunch as we toasted our sandwiches over an open fire

"Right down there," and he pointed to the river, "right there is the Rifkin Rapids. Sometimes in the night of a spring full moon you can see the ghost of the Girl of Rifkin Rapids, or maybe hear her cry outwhere she drowned."

The others looked down in wonder. I told George I didn't believe in ghosts. Besides, I'd never heard of one that cried out in the night.

"All right. Don't believe me. But my Dad sure enough saw her and heard her all to once't. Why I even heard her cry in the night myself."

We had a few more minutes to go till noonin' was over, so George rolled himself a smoke of Bull Durham, lit it with a glowing stick from the fire and the four of us sat there that chilly day in September while he told the story.

It was back in the days when they cut logs in the winter and skidded them down by horse, mule and oxen to where they could be put on the ice of the frozen Sacandaga and driven down stream to the mills on the Sacandaga when the snow and ice melted and made high waters.

Short Leg Cousins, who had had a busted leg heal up shorter than the other, lived upriver with his growing daughter, his wife having died from lung fever. Short Leg now and then did all kinds of jobs around the valley. But in the winter he made up a raft of dry spruce logs and erected a little shack on it for him and Elva, the girl, to live in. They used the raft to go down river from place to place in log-drivin' time. Elva, a right pretty girl who was not yet married, did the cookin' for the meals of the river men and loggers on the log drive.

Well, it happened on the night of the full moon. The fires had long been lit on shore and were now a bed of glowing red coals. The men were fed, the tin plates and cups washed and stacked in the cubby on the raft. Elva and Shorty were asleep in the raft house, for mornin' meal came early. But, even though the moon hung big and bright in the sky, one of the sudden valley thunder boomers come roaring along over the river waters. That wind and heavy rain churned up the wasters and sloshed the logs that had edged to shore in shallow places and in eddies. It simply raised hell!

Some said later it was a Devil's Wind in search of souls. Well, if that's what it was, it sure was a winner that night. With the lashing around of the wind-driven waters and the sloshing, bumping and grinding of the logs, the rope mooring the raft to a big boulder at the shore line either got broke or tore loose. In a terrible, wild mess, the raft and the logs were forced downriver and right through those Rifkin Rapids.

Sad to say, the raft got torn apart in that there melee of wind, logs, rocks and wild waters. The body of Short Leg was found the next morn. It was all battered and broke up. A mess. The body of poor beautiful Elva was never found, even though the rivermen and loggers searched for days.

Some said the girl's body had been torn to bits by the logs and rocks in the rapids. The big pike fish and moss-backed snapper turtles ate the flesh and crunched the bones. But some old-timey fellers—and some of them was part Indian—and they sure enough knew, said, "Sacandag, the Great Spirit of the river, claimed the girl."

And, once again, George told us that even he had

heard in the night the lonesome call of the spirit of that drowned girl call out. "Who will save me? Who? Who?"

Well, back to work we went on the project of the first dam. But I can't let the story end there. For I too heard that call in the night. It was after WWII. I was working on the construction project of the second dam. I held many jobs there. One was night fireman on the 11:00 PM to 7:00 AM shift, six nights a week.

Several nights after midnight, the witching hour, as I worked there near the old Rifkin Rapids I heard from far off an eerie cry. "Who? Who? Who?"

I've oft times wondered, did I just hear the cry of a hunting owl or was it truly the poor lost soul of Elva, the Girl at Rifkin Rapids?

HE HAD A CURSE ON HIM!

Poor Ol' George was accused of throwing a witch woman into the icy, cold waters of the river where she drowned. He said he did it in self defense. One newspaper of the outside the valley wrote, "Did Bible Figure in Witch Slaying?"

Monk Karol said that Poor Ol' George was some sort of a shirt-tailed relation of his, a distant great-uncle or some such. George had been sort of addle-minded as a boy growing up, but he was very religious. George had done odd jobs for that witch lady to earn money. All went well until the night of Halloween. Then somehow or other, the lady and her hired hand got into an argument that led to the lady in the river in the early days of Croweville.

Monk said the full facts never did come out, for the lady was dead and Poor Ol' George slipped deep into religion. It seems that George claimed the woman was a witch and some folks around the area did also. George claimed that the witch woman had put a spell on him. The giving of the witch to the power of the river was like a sacrifice in the Scriptures.

George had tried a lock of hair from a black dog to break his spell. He had even put tar on the doorstep of the witch to catch the feet of the devil. But the witch had laughed at George and taunted him. So he choked her some and then placed her in the river.

Many local people sided with Ol' George. But Ol' George came before the Justice of the Peace. He had George put in the State Crazy House out at Utica.

WAS IT A
VISION OR A DREAM?

Pat Diskin said his Uncle Patrick Diskin, through some unexplained strange psychic power, was able to bring a murderer to arrest and jail.

Uncle Patrick had to go to the Fish House Village to see a lawyer for settlement of a timber claim he was selling. The buyer was there. The papers were signed and Patrick received his money. Then Patrick had supper in a small eatin' place and went to the Fish House Hotel to get a room for the night before the long trip home by horse and wagon.

The hotel man told him there were no rooms, it was all filled up. Just then the hotel man's wife came in and said that it was now snowing. Patrick told them that now he sure had to get a bed. He couldn't drive twenty miles at night in a snowstorm in a horse and wagon. They agreed. The woman told her husband, "You'll have to rent him that last room."

Patrick said, "Please. Anything."

So they gave him a key to a room on the second floor and the woman went up with him to put sheets on the bed. There were a couple of folded blankets on a chair. Patrick told the lady there was a strange smell in the room She told him it was musty as it had been locked up.

There was a narrow glass door that fronted on a small wooden balcony. Patrick opened that door for fresh air and stepped out on the balcony and looked over a low railing on the street below. The air was fresh, cold and it was snowing some. He went back in

the room and was thankful that he had a bed for the night despite the unpleasant odor. Then he thought, "This is the smell of death, of blood. I've smelled it before."

He blew out the light of the coal oil lamp and went to bed and fell asleep. After some sleep he was awakened by a strong feeling of trouble. He thought of his money which he had in a small sack beneath his pillow. He felt for it. It was there. But he struck a Lucifer and lit the lamp, turned it low. He settled down, but with eyes wide open he saw a figure climb over the porch railing, open the glass door and enter his room. There was enough light to see and a feller that looked like a small Canadian with clean-shaven face and with a twist at the left corner of his lip. Most all local men had hair on their faces.

The face looked evil. Patrick seemed to be frozen, unable to move. The man came to the bed, he had a knife in one hand. He stood above Patrick and plunged it into his chest. Not once, but twice. The murderer, for that is what he was, looked around the room, went to the unused fireplace, crouched down and stuck the knife up the chimney. Then Patrick just passed out, or went back into a sleep.

He awoke in the morning. There were no wounds in his chest. He decided he'd had a strange dream and sat on the edge of the bed. But now there was the smell, the odor, unpleasant, stronger than the night before. Patrick pulled his pants on, for he'd slept in his long underwear. The dream, if that was what it was, was very clear, in his mind.

But the oil lamp was still lit, turned down low, but lit. He was sure that he'd turned it off when he went to bed. He must have really awakened, felt for his money and re-lit the oil lamp as he remembered. He was awake and saw the man. Whether he was real or a spirit, but he had seen him. That strong odor, that was real and not just a musty smell as the lady said. So, he looked the room over, then tore the bedding apart—no, she had put that on clean. He'd seen her do it.

Then he turned the straw-filled mattress over. The underside was soaked with blood and that was the smell. He looked at it and knew he had seen the night before he'd been in that room. That was when the attack on whoever who had been in that bed before him took place. Quick-like he put on his wool stockings, boots, shirt and coat and took his money bag and hurried down stairs. He faced the owner about the bloody mattress and told of the vision he had seen in the night.

"Yes," the owner admitted, there had been a murder the other night. A lumberman was stabbed to the death in that room. The owner shrugged. He should have changed the mattress. Maybe it was wrong to rent the room in such a condition, but Patrick had insisted—so? Then Patrick asked who was the local law thereabouts. The constable was also the blacksmith, he'd be in his shop soon.

Patrick went to the little eatin' place. As he was eating his ham and eggs he saw a short, clean shaven Frenchman sitting near him. The feller had a swelling on his lip. Patrick watched him close. He knew for sure that was the same man that had appeared to him the night before in his room because when the Frenchman was served his ham and eggs the feller picked his knife up from the table next his plate, he held the knife as if he was stabbing the ham that his fork was holding steady on his plate. That was just the way the murderer held and used the knife last night when he stabbed at the figure on the bed. He wasn't holding the knife to cut his ham like most folks do, with the first finger along the top of the back of the knife and sort of use it as a saw to cut the ham.

Patrick at once went to see the constable-blacksmith at his shop, and told his story. The constable rubbed his chin and listened to the story and said, "I think you are crazy, talking about a dream or what you call a vision. Ain't no such things. And a French Canada feller cuttin' up his ham on his plate. Crazy notions you fellers from the valley always has. But—the man is dead. We sure don't have no idee who did that stabbin'. Well, let's go look at that there chimney before we get all shook up."

The constable removed his leather apron, buckled on a belt with a holstered revolver, then called to another man to go with them. At the hotel room the constable squatted down before the fireplace. Sure enough, up in the flue, wedged in the damper, was a hunting knife with a dried bloodstained blade.

They went to the eatin' place, then to the grog shop. The constable took the Frenchman with no trouble for he was surprised. Back at the blacksmith shop, they showed the prisoner the knife and Patrick told his story again. The prisoner admitted he'd killed the man and hid the knife just like Patrick said he saw it done in his dream or vision. In those days, if you admitted you did a crime, why you musta done-done it!

The Frenchman said the lumberman had punched him in the mouth over an argument about a girl. It was in the house in Big Vly, owned by a young witch. She told fortunes, sold drinks and had a couple other girls there. More on that another time. Anyway the Frenchman went to County Court for trial and was jailed.

Over the years I have sometimes wondered. . .

Did the murdered victim appear before Patrick on the bed in the room to have the happening disclose the murderer? Or was it a time dimension thing if there is such a thing? Or does a crime remain in some form where it happened? Anyway, something happened and a man was killed, another man went to jail for that death.

Like I've sometimes said—strange things happened in the Valley in the 'Dacks!

THE GHOST LIGHT OF THE OLD LOG CHURCH

Someone told Mark Twain that the world was coming to an end. He responded, "That's okay—we can get along without it."

That's what Len Gordon said. Then he added, "Jesus promised us that a new world would come one day. And believe you me, that's just what is happening to our valley. A new world is coming upon the lands with this dam."

Len was a tree feller, a lumberjack, one of the large crew of men clearing all trees and brush from the thousands of acres to be flooded. He told this story:

Built of logs in the 1800's, it was known as the "Fellowship Church." Emory Page, a lumber baron and self-named preacher Man, he built the church at White Oak Cove. There were troubles at the Church and the name was changed to "Fellowship Center." It was later spoken of as the "Spooky Church" on the river.

Emory also had a house and a saw mill nearby at Shady Brook. Emory was strict with his family. Then his daughter ran off with a man buying bridge timbers at the sawmill. This caused Emory to act wildly and blame the Devil for taking his daughter. After a bit the poor girl, not much more than a child herself, came back home asking her father's forgiveness and admitting she was with child. The stern father, hidebound in his beliefs, would not forgive the girl and ordered her to sleep in the woodshed at the rear of the church.

After a week or so, the unhappy girl hung herself in the doorway of the log church. Two sawmill workers on their way to work, found the girl's body hanging in the doorway. They tried to cut it down, hoping to revive the girl. The rope slipped, the body and the men fell to the floor at the church entrance. The men ran to the sawmill for help, which got there too late to save the girl.

The girl and her unborn child were buried in a small buryin' ground alongside the church. Following that a strange eerie light was seen nights at the church door. This went on for awhile and was seen by several persons. It was called "the tortured soul." The father, on Sundays, continued to denounce the Devil. But folks stopped coming to the log church, now called "Spooky Church".

One Sunday morn in spring, a day of sunshine and growing life, there was no one sitting on the benches in the church as Emory Page entered to give a sermon. He must have felt abandoned. The Fellowship had ended with his rejection of his very own daughter and the child she bore, and the tragic end of her life.

Emory Page hung himself on an overhanging branch of the large White Oak Tree. He, too, was placed in the buryin' ground. But his widow insisted that his body not be placed next to the grave of the daughter and the child that never came into the world. Her love for her husband had turned to hate when he banished the girl to the woodshed and death.

Missus Emory sold the forest lands on the mountain, the sawmill and her home. But first she gave the log church, buryin' ground and 25 acres of land to two men at act as trustees. A new church group was started and a minister was hired after a stone rectory was built for him to live in. The spooky light was still seen at night at the church, but folk had gotten used to it. Attendance at the church began to grow, despite that strange light seen in the dark of night.

Len Grodon also told me that in the late 18 and 90's,

a flash flood in the river damaged the church and swept away a one-room school that had been built on church grounds. So the trustees sold off about 23 acres of land, so only two remained for the church. The church was fixed and new chinking and daubing of clay used to replace the old between the logs. A new school was started, but a bolt of lightning struck the white oak tree and the church. The log church burned to the ground. The ghost light was seen no more!

THE SCREAMING SKULL

We were at Jimtown on the Sacandaga River. We sat down next a wonderful boiling spring. The sands in the spring were white as sugar and there, moving on top the sands were tiny bits of black from broken up dead leaves and such. The black stuff swirled and moved around and made all sorts of patterns. The water was as pure as could be and earth cold.

I said to my companion, "What a great spot! With this view of the river and this spring water to drink, I'm surprised no one ever built on this knoll."

Someone did once, he said.

Long years ago there had been a house there. Now and then someone would come to the empty house but they always left in a hurry. It seems the previous owners, before they disappeared had a bare human skull hanging in a corner of one room. When anyone reached toward it or tried to take it down, there was an awful screaming, an unearthly screaming. An invisible force would knock the person to the floor. Then a very severe storm would sweep downa from the skies. There would be fierce winds, thunder boomers, streaks of lightning and heavy rains. If anyone tried to touch the skull in winter, there'd be an almost blizzard-like condition, wild winds, heavy snows and cold—severe cold.

Finally some one burned the building with the eerie skull to the ground. Only the name of that spot in the valley remained—the Hill of the Screaming Skull!

THE MISSING LEG

Wally told us that his great uncle Lymus Wood of the little hamlet called "Dandy's Shanty" was a riverman. But one spring evening, just at dusk, he was riding some logs down river on the spring run when a sudden valley storm made the waters rise and the heavy winds churned up the waters real bad. Lymus, even though he wore caulked boots lost his footing on the log and he fell into the river.

The angry waters, the wind, and the bumping, crashing logs were too much for mortal man to come through in one piece. Lymus had his right leg crushed between some logs. When fellow river drivers got him to shore, they feared for his life. He was rushed, by horse and buggy, miles away to the hospital at Broadalbin.

The doctors saved the feller's life but had to amputate the damaged leg. The lumber company he worked for sent Lymus down to Albany where he was fitted with a nice wooden leg and Lymus became right proud of that there fake leg. He would take if off and hold it like a little girl does her doll. He had someone bring him a bottle of furniture polish and a small bottle of Iodine. If the leg got a nick, scratch, or whatever, Lymus would put iodine on it to darken the scratch then use furniture polish and rub and polish till it shone right smart. Why he even had the blacksmith at Osborn's Bridge village make a copper shoe like to fit the bottom of the leg so water wouldn't damage it, or any kind of wood worms get in it.

Lymus, he liked to hunt. He always had, and always

would. But, one fall day, up on Moonshine Mountain, he slipped, fell off a ledge to the ground. No one ever knew if it was the sudden stop when he hit the ground killed him or the pack of wolves that ate him up. Those critters left nothin' but the skull and some other bones and the wood leg. That's how they come to figure the original owner of the skull and bones was Lymus. Because of that there wood leg. After all, wasn't no one else around the valley or the mountains that wore a wooden leg with a copper bottom to it. The skull and bones were placed in a wooden soap box and buried in the local buryin' ground. The wood leg they gave to Missus Nan Wood as the last earthly remains of her husband.

It had been a shock to Nan, but she kept working. Some women in the valley worked at home, sewing leather gloves for the glove factory. They sent a feller around to country folks, in a horse and wagon. The women folk sewed the gloves by hand. The man picked 'em up and paid for the work.

As I say, Nan she did all right in her work but other times, she spent much of her thoughts on Lymus and some of her time with that there wood leg. She held it, petted it, was even heard talking to it. That was until she had a rack made over the fire-mantel and hung the leg there like a man does a deer or wolf head. Only the leg had no glass eyes.

Well, a bad storm came down the river one night. Same kind of storm that cost Lymus his natural leg. The storm wakened Nan. She sat up in bed. There was a flash of lightning and Nan saw Lymus standin' on one leg, straight as a locust fence post. She was scared. Then there was another flash of lightning and Lymus hopped over to the side of the bed, leant over and said, "Nan, I'll need my store-bought leg, so I can get away from the wolves."

Nan must have passed out, 'cause next thing she

knew it was morning. She thought she musta had a bad dream, made some breakfast, ate, started to sew gloves. A neighbor lady from upriver came to borrow some heavy thread till her supplies came. Nan made coffee for the two of them and told about her dream. The neighbor lady said that there had been a storm during the night and she didn't think it was a dream. She persuaded Nan to walk down river with her to visit the witch of Brimstone Hill. The witch, a granny woman gave them herb tea to drink. Nan told her story of the night happening.

This lady was what was called a white witch. She never did things that might scare or harm a person. She only did good things. Cast spells, told fortunes, birthed babies, gave amulets and bags of herbs to wear around the neck to ward off evil, colored pebbles, herb teas, potions, cure-all prayers, advice and such to help folks.

So this white witch, she tells Nan that the spirit of her dead hubby Lymus is wandering around in the spirit world. Restless. He feels lost without the leg he had learned to use and love. He needs to feel whole again even beyond death. She told Nan that they must set Lymus at rest, and that in turn would set Nan at ease. She believed she knew how.

The three women went to the sawmill and talked to one of the men who had found the skull, bones and wooden leg in the forest. The man agreed with their plan. He got some burlap bags, went to the house at Dandy's Shanty, took the wooden leg down from the wall, wrapped it in burlap, took it to the buryin' ground and buried the leg next to the box with the skull and bones.

The next severe storm that came to the valley and the storms after that never bothered Nan Wood again. The missing leg had been returned to the owner. May God rest his soul!

READING THE STARS

Could the witches in the valley foretell the future of people from the position of the stars, planets and other heavenly bodies at the time of a person's birth? I guess people have argued about that for hundreds of years, long before the valley was first settled by non-Indians in the 1700's. Those witch ladies didn't go by the fancy name of Astrology and Astrologists. They just called it "fortune telling by the stars."

A man met the witch of Brimstone Hill at the store in Huntsville. He knew her and put a silver coin in her hand and asked her if he had a good day coming up? The lady knew him, knew he was a Taurus and told him to be very careful that day. Take extra care and guard against accidents.

The man laughed in front of the folks on the porch and said he was only joking as he really didn't believe it, as it was all just hogwash. However, as he walked down the dirt road toward the sawmill where he worked a runaway horse and wagon charged down on him. He was able to leap to one side, but the wagon struck him and knocked him down. The people from the store started to run to him. He got up, waved his hands, yelled, "I'm okay!" and proceeded to the mill.

At the sawmill everything was moving smoothly for a while. Then a load of logs on a dray pulled on the mill yard and as they started to loosen the chains, one chain snapped. The logs tumbled to the ground and that same man the witch had warned received a broken leg.

Another man was told one evening by the same witch lady to be very careful of accidents the next day. He was a blacksmith. His morning started off smooth as usual. Then a drover brought an ox to the shop to have new shoes put on. That's right! Working oxen were shod with metal shoes same as horses. But the ox is a bovine and has split hooves. So each foot has to have two shoes put on. A total of eight shoes per ox. The hoof which grows is clipped, filed and the shoes fitted and nailed on. I once drove oxen so I know.

A horse will generally stand still to be shod. Oh, sometimes a skittish horse needs a man or boy to hold the halter or headstall to keep it from moving or fidgeting, as the smith lifts one foot at a time and holds it between his knees to put the old shoe, trim and shape the hoof and nail the shoe on. You cannot do that with an ox. A broad canvas or leather sling has to be placed under the ox belly and a lift pole raises the ox off the floor so the feet could be worked on. The end of the stout hardwood pole is secured in place with a tie-down.

Well, Smitty got that ox on the sling and the animal off the ground. As the man began to work on the feet, something happened and the ox crashed down on the blacksmith. The drover who was there quick untangled things, tied the ox outside and helped the Smith. But the Smith got a fractured skull, busted ribs and a broken leg. He really believed in fortune telling by the stars after that.

The same with the chap who was hired to paint the church at Conklinville. Like some other fellers, he tried to joke and make sport of the witch when he saw her in the store. But even if someone was making fun and he put a piece of silver in her palm she'd seriously tell a quick fortune. Money was money and even witch ladies had to eat.

Well, the painter feller said later that the witch lady had told him to avoid high places the next day. But, in a spirit of bravado, he picked the very next morn to paint the steeple. The ladder slipped. Paint pot and painter landed on the ground. He got a broken arm from his fall from a high place!

Me? Well, I do read the horoscope column in the morning newspaper. Do you? Do I pay it any mind? You can just bet I do! I remember a Sunday morn the paper told us Gemini people to be very careful of travel. A drunken driver totaled our car. Christine received a broken arm and other injuries. The first ten days of my hospital stay I was unconscious and in a coma.

Yes, I follow the astrology forecasts. You can bet your favorite Lucky Star I do!

THE WITCH WOLF

Baynard Kirkwood told How his great uncle had married a witch but did not care about that at first because she was so pretty and happy a person.

Back before the turn of the century, Uncle Jake Silversides was hunting near the old cabin at the foot of Burnt Wolf Peak. He came upon a wolf on the stream bank. The animal saw him and whirled as Jake raised his gun, not quick enough to shoot. The critter darted right toward the old cabin that stood doorless at the edge of the creek and Jake followed.

The wolf glared at him from the darkness of the cabin in the doorway. Jake couldn't believe his eyes, it was not a regular grey wolf or even a rare black wolf. This creature had a dark stripe down the back. He knew at once that it was what was spoken of as a streaked wolf, The kind that was associated with witches.

The animal whirled back into the cabin as Jake raised his gun. Jake, gun at the ready, stepped toward the door opening. There was a movement and into the opening stepped a lovely girl, the most lovely female he had ever seen, with hair black as a raven's wing. And, wonder of wonders she wore no clothes, not a stitch. Jake was stunned. He was speechless before such beauty.

The girl spoke, telling him she needed help. She had come there with friends to pick late-growing blueberries. The day was so nice she'd slipped off her clothes and went swimming in the waters of the creek. But her friends left, taking her clothes, maybe as a joke. Would he help her?

Jake looked at the unfortunate girl and came to his senses. He took off his coat, gave it to her and told her he would take her to the home of his aunt who would help her. The girl took his coat and put it on. It was large and covered her fairly well. Then she laughed in a happy way that made Jake happy.

Jake did not know that the girl was a witch. Because of the danger from the rifle, she had slipped her wolf skin off and appeared as a pretty girl. Jake just forgot all about the wolf and took the pretty girl to the cabin of his aunt. The girl told her story. The aunt gave the girl a dress and fed them both at the kitchen table. The girl said she was visiting from Tamarack Swamp in the Big Vly. She was happy and full of smiles. By then it was getting dark and the aunt told the girl she would have to stay the night in an extra room. In the morning they would see about getting the loan of a horse and wagon to take her home. Jake would return in the morn.

On the way home Jake met the Indian pow wow man. Jake was so happy about the girl he told the old man what had happened. He was in Love!

The old Indian became worried. He told Jake that he was under a spell and if he did not take care, the Devil would have his soul. The streaked wolf he had seen was a female witch-wolf who could shed the wolf skin. She had become a pretty, happy girl to lure Jake under her control. Jake was in grave danger. That girl could return to the cabin at any time and put on the skin of the witch wolf. Jake should not see the girl again.

But the young chap had lost his heart and head to that beautiful, laughing, happy girl. He had to have her for his own. He asked what could be done. The pow wow shook his head and told him that if his twisted mind truly wanted the girl that he saw, then he must get a lantern, a hammer and some nails. He must rush to the cabin and seek the wolf pelt, before the girl got there. When Jake found the pelt he had to stretch it out and nail it to a wall. Then the witch could not get back in the wolf skin. She would have to stay as the girl and could not leave. If that was what he wanted then he would have the girl—and plenty of trouble!

Jake thanked the old man, rushed home and got the things that he needed and went to the old cabin. Sure enough, he found the wolf skin and nailed the pelt to a wall. He then returned home, went to bed but could not sleep, turning and tossing all night, thinking of the lovely girl creature that would be his and thinking of the nailed to the wall wolf skin that would keep her a lovely girl.

The next morn he rushed to the home of his aunt to find her and the girl were having coffee. The girl looked sad, not all smiles. He asked her if she would like to stay and marry him or if he should go get a horse and wagon to take her home to the swamp? The girl told him that there was no need now for her to go. She might as well stay there.

Stay she did. The two of them moved into their own cabin. She would not wed him, gave him but little love, smiled no more and seemed to become an old hag, always screaming and scolding him. There were no more happy smiles. Conditions became very bad between them. Finally Jake went to see the old pow wow doctor and took him some gifts of chickens and home made cheese.

The old man listened to Jake's troubles, gave the young feller some sort of wild herb tea, said some prayers and then told Jake that on the day of the next full moon he must return to the cabin at Burnt Wolf Creek and remove the wolfskin from the wall and take it home. At nightfall he was to spread the skin on the ground outside his cabin and wet it with a pail of water so that it no longer would be hard and stiff as skins become.

The young fellow did that. He and the witch girl went to bed. Sometime in the night he woke. The girl was gone. He went to the window, the light of the full moon bathed the countryside and crickets were chirping, an owl hooted. He could not see the wolfskin on the ground. The next morning he must have gone to the river for a pail of water to make coffee. Later someone found the water pail on the riverbank. Two days later the body of Jake Silversides was found in the river.

He had loved and lost!

PART THREE:

WHITE HORSE FROM HELL

THE WITCH OF
HOO DOO RIDGE

The story I was told about Ernest Pearson of Little Bear Springs was that several times a witch woman turned him into a horse on nights of the full moon and rode him up and down the valley.

He'd wake up of a morning all tired out and sweaty and his legs scratched up from black berry briars and cat claw vines. The last time it happened he was frothing at the mouth and breathing and snorting like a horse. So his wife sent a boy for the pow wow doctor.

The pow wow man agreed with Ernest that he had really been out at night and probably ridden by a witch. He didn't believe it was a wild nightmare. The pow wow said some prayers, gave Ernest some herbs to drink and treated his scratches. Then he gave Ernest some directions of what to do to free himself from the power the witch held over him.

Ernest took a shotgun shell, took out the wadding and the lead shot. Next he took a silver dollar and cut it into pieces with his axe. He put the bits of silver in the shell instead of the lead shot and capped it with the wadding. Then he tacked a picture the pow wow had drawn on an old paper store sack of an old woman onto the side of the barn. The pow wow said some special prayers as Ernest shot his gun at the picture.

A couple days later an old woman died in her shack at Hoo Doo Ridge. A lady friend of hers that tended her told that the woman had strange injuries, like those made by gunshot, in her legs, chest and stomach.

THE WHITE GHOST HORSE

I remember a story about a white horse. It started with Old Hicks and his livery stable at Osborn Bridge.

A Gypsy band came along the river and sold Mister Hicks a fine-standing white horse. The only thing seemed to be wrong with the horse was that its feet were not shod. So Hicks got Flynn the Blacksmith to shoe the horse. When the job was done, Mister Flynn told Hicks that the horse had tender feet.

Then a feller from Denton's Corners rented the horse and a buggy. As he started to drive the horse through the covered bridge, a black cat, chased by a black dog ran across in front of the horse. That was a bad sign. The horse got spooked, whirled around, took the bit in its teeth and ran away on the road to Northville. The scared horse finally slowed down in the soft dirt of the road and the driver finally got it under control.

But, even so, the horse could not be turned around with the reins held from the seat. So the driver got down and went to the horse's head to take a hold of the bridle and turn horse and buggy around. The horse tossed his head and bit the man on the hand, started off and a buggy wheel ran over a foot of the man. The last the man saw of the horse and buggy, they were going across an open field into a patch of woods.

The man sat down on a split rail fence, concerned about his injuries. A drover with a yoke of oxen came along the road, heading for Osborn Bridge. He had the injured man get in his cart and took him to Osborn Bridge. There, he told the livery man his story and the livery man got a pow wow man to doctor the horse bite and fix the broken toes. The livery man was worried about his white horse and buggy and got several men to go searching.

They found the busted-up buggy in the woods,. Further in, they found the reins and gear from the horse, that was now running free. Free it was for weeks. It was seen day and night running the roads, fields and woods. The critter was even seen in the Big Vly. The livery man put out a reward for the horse.

Then one evening a man living in the Vly saw the white horse. Such a person living out there was called a "swamper." The swamper got some friends and with ropes tried to catch the animal for the cash reward. But the horse eluded them and ran into the marsh. It tried to cross one of the quivering bogs and the men saw the horse sucked slowly into the bottomless muck of the bog. Word was sent to the livery man about the death of his horse.

But soon stories began to be told about a big white horse that was seen thundering and galloping like a ghost on the moonlit roads. It scared livestock and people and caused horse-pulled wagons to veer off the roads and smash up. Some folks got hurt. One man was so scared that the hair on his head stood up stiff like the quills on a porky pine and never did settle down.

A witch woman from near Beecher's Hollow saw the "White Horse from Hell," as she described it. She said the vision was the work of the Devil. The Devil had been in the live horse and getting shod had infuriated the creature. The only way the Devil could be gotten out of it was if the ghost was treated in a certain way.

So a couple of venturesome young fellers went to talk to the witch after the ghost horse scared some of their sheep in a pasture. The woolies ran off a steep bank into a gully and a dozen of the flock were killed. The witch lady told the young men that the only thing to stop the horse was to fire a silver bullet into it. That would let the Devil out of the ghost horse and allow it to return to the bog where it had drowned in the quagmire, there to rest in peace.

She instructed the two fellers to remove the wad and shot from a couple of shotgun shells and replace the shot with pieces of cut-up silver dollars. They did that and replaced the wads to hold the silver pieces in the shells. Then, for a couple weeks, they prowled the countryside. Finally, on the night of the full moon they saw the ghost horse and shot it. They saw the apparition stagger and then walk slowly to the bogs. They followed and saw the critter sink into the black muck of the bog.

The white ghost horse was never seen again. The Devil had left it and the poor creature finally rested in peace.

And that was another happening in the Sacandaga Valley.

THUNDERCLAP HILL

Red Barney of Elm Tree Hill got drunk so many times it was pitiful. He wasted all his money on drink. This made it hard for his wife and children. The last time he came home drunk, he staggered in through the door when his wife opened it. Then, he was so dead drunk that he just fell on the floor.

The Missus tried to get him up to get him to bed. He was no help at all.

"Oh my head hurts. I'm sick I'll stay here," was all she said.

Missus had lost all patience with the lout. She says, "All right, you just lay there like a dog."

Red Barney moaned, "Oh I'm sick. I'm gonna die."

She replied, "Die then, damn you! And let the Devil take you."

The next morning when she got up and went to him he was still on the floor by the door. She tried to waken him, then realized that he was stone cold dead.

On his forehead there was a black mark, looked like a single footprint of a goat. Some folks that saw it told around that was the mark of the Devil. So folks talked around about the Footprint of Satan on Red Barney. Some neighbor went down to Conklingville and brought the barber and one of his pine boxes back in a wagon, so they could lay Red out. The barber even fixed his long red hair so it covered the mark on the forehead.

Folks sat around waitin' for the preacher to arrive and give a little service. Then the already-dug grave out back by the apple tree would receive the last remains of

Red Barney. But, before the preacher could arrive, a boomer of a storm come rushing down the valley. A blazing streak of lightning hit the house and there came the most tremendous clap of thunder. Folks rushed out the house into the rain and back to the barn for shelter. The house on Elm Tree Hill made a wondrous fire. It burned to the ground and consumed everything, including the body of Red Barney, who was taken by the Devil, indeed.

Thereafter, folks called that place Thunderclap Hill!

THE WITCH OF DEADWOOD CLEARING

Constable Josh Winchell was told that a girl had been killed by a panther at Dead Wood Clearing at the cabin of Tess Berry. Josh got three or four men to go with him to the clearing, which was really a jumble of dead trees caused by a terrible wind storm years before.

Granny's cabin had been built near a small spring, not far from the river. When the men arrived by boat, they found the body of the girl in some bushes near the spring. She had been sixteen years old and worked as a servant. She had been terribly cut, slashed and mauled. Josh, great, great uncle of Wash Winchell who was telling the story, had also been a farmer, log cutter and drove logs down the river in the spring drive. Josh was also a hunter. He was not satisfied that a panther had killed the girl. From what he saw it did not look right. The bounty on the varmints had reduced their numbers around Dailey Creek. Furthermore, the body and the surrounding ground upset his mind. He was not satisfied.

So Josh began to question Tess Berry very strongly. The old lady who was a midwife and granny lady kept telling him she knew nothing, only that she had found the dead girl. Then one of the men in the group, who was part Indian, Maurice St. John, told Josh he did not believe the girl had been killed there, as there was not much blood. Nor did he think a panther's claws did the job. He thought it looked like knife cuts. He and Josh both tried to get Tess to tell them more.

Tess was not only a granny woman who helped at birthin's and a herb doctor, she was spoken of by some people as a black witch, a practitioner of evil witchcraft. A white witch practiced only good for people, whereas a black witch went for evil practices and spells.

Tess was believed, it was said in whispers, to prey on people—sort of what is now called extortion—by filling them with fears and threats. She demanded money or gifts like a goat, calf or a shoat or chickens. It was said that anyone who didn't give to her or opposed her wishes, fell sick. Some even died.

Constable Josh and Maurice could not shake the old lady's story that she had seen no one, heard no noise, only found the girl dead where they saw her. The two men and the others could find no clues and were very mystified. This was the worst case that the Township Fence Viewers had ever been called in to settle. Before it had been breaking up a fight, or locking up a drunken lumberjack, chicken stealing or an argument over a farm fence or a property line in the woods. (Years later I myself had to rely on the Fence Viewers in several disputes. Some old timers believed that a line of old blaze marks on trees was well and good, but that they could cut over onto the neighbor's side for as far as they could toss an axe.)

Anyway, the girl's body was taken across the river by boat to the little town of Concord and buried in the church yard. Josh had told Tess that he did not believe her but could not prove it. He'd keep his eye on her.

Witchcraft, or magic, or trickery, call it what you will, can be dangerous. Things began to happen to the constable, little annoying things. A calf wandered off or was stolen. A cat was found dead on some blackberry bushes as if tossed there. A dog's leg was broken. Chickens were missing, there was a snake in the milk pail and such like.

Then word came that Tess the witch had another

young hired girl working for her. She was cooking, washing dishes and clothes, drawing and lugging water from the spring, chopping and carrying wood for the stove, milking goats, making goat cheese.

Dead Wood Clearing was on the south side of the river near the mouth of Dailey Creek. There were only remote scattered cabins and shacks in the many miles between Batchellerville and Conklinville, each of which had a bridge across the river. There was just a rough, dirt, wagon track along the river. People living along there had to use a boat or cross on winter ice.

One day Tess' hired girl came across the river in a rowboat to see the constable. She wanted to report the chickens of Tess had been stolen and she brought some goat milk cheese to exchange for some eggs. Barter system was common in those days. She was given some eggs. After she was gone it was discovered that a hat of Josh's, hanging by the door, was missing. It was decided the girl took it for Tess. In those days a witch liked to get a few hairs, fingernail parings or a personal item of their intended victim. Josh began to feel lazy, weak and sick. Tess had placed a spell on him.

Then Josh received word that the second girl was dead at Tess' place over in Dead Wood Clearing. As sick as he was, Josh got some men and they crossed the river in couple of boats. As they rowed across they saw a plume of smoke rising toward the sky ahead of them. When they beached the boats they saw the log cabin of Tess Berry was a mass of flames. The dead girl was found all cut up. Later, in the ruins of the cabin, they found what they believed was the burned skull of Tess Berry, the black witch. They buried it right there.

The dead girl was taken across the river and given a Christian burial, same as the first girl. Years later when the dam was put in the Sacandaga River, all the graves that could be located were dug up and any remains moved to higher ground and a record kept as well as possible of the relocations.

The health of Josh improved. Later it was learned that the second girl had had a boy friend who intended to marry her. He'd now fled, it was believed, toward Canada. The belief was that when the young man heard of the death of his girl, he had killed Tess the witch. Then the young man burned the cabin and Tess.

Another sad happening in the Valley, that of Dead Wood Clearing.

HER HAND WAS BURNED

Wally Underwood owned several horses. He owned work horses that he rented out in teams to loggers, and singles for skidding. There were road horses to pull his carriages and buggies, a couple of trotting horses to race in the county fairs and some saddle horses. He owned a big farm, a sawmill, was believed to have a lot of money, had good looks and was unmarried. He always took his horses for hoof trimming and to be shod at the forge of Wilbur Flynn the Smitty at Osborn Bridge Village.

Wilbur had just hired a helper, a young chap name of Cliff Harris who had just come from working the Season at Saratoga Springs Racetrack. Cliff and his wife Ethel rented a house the other side of the covered bridge in Denton's Corners. Ethel was a beautiful girl, black hair, lovely smile with white teeth and jet black eyes.

Even though Ethel was a young married woman, Wally fell in love with her the first time he saw her, when he brought a horse to be shod. From then on, he found reasons to bring a horse to the forge, every few days, in hopes that Ethel was there to see her husband Cliff, having carried lunch to him. After a time or two, at noontime the young wife-girl would ask Wally to have a cup of hot tea with them.

While the three young people sat there, Blacksmith Wilbur Flynn, who was much older, would go to his nearby home, have a real dinner with his wife and then take a nap. The three young people got along well together. Too well, I was told. When Cliff went back to his work in the shop, his wife and Wally, the horse owner, became real friendly. Wally soon told Ethel that he loved her and asked her to go away with him. She told him that she couldn't do that. But during the night of the next full moon she might come to his farm and spend a few hours with him as a lark.

Wally went home with his horse. He was probably the happiest man in the valley as he thought of raven-haired Ethel. She was all he could think of for the next few days. He couldn't sleep. His thoughts were on that girl and what she might mean to him. Finally he said to his cat, "I am bewitched," and went to sleep.

The next day Wally didn't take a horse to the smitty, but fussed around not doing much, his mind on the girl. Finally as it grew dark and the full moon rose slowly over the mountain he fell asleep in a chair. About midnight, he awoke to a sound and saw the beautiful Ethel in the doorway. She held out her hand and he arose. She kissed him and led him out to the yard where she had two saddled black mares. They mounted and rode through the moonlit night to Grass Springs, an open glade near the river, surrounded by trees.

There were people dancing on the grass. Wally saw a man sitting on a boulder at the edge of the field playing a wild dance on a fiddle. Ethel fitted into Wally's arms and they danced as a couple. They had drinks that were set out on an oak stump near the fiddler.

Then Wally began to notice something about that the fiddler. He seemed to have a pair of horns on his head like a goat and his eyes were eyes of fire. Then the horned fiddler told Wally that by taking that drink, Wally had given his soul to Ethel and in turn to him, the Devil himself!

Wally was under the spell of the drink, which may have been jimson weed, a hallucinogenic substance— too much of which can bring on death. The next thing

Wally knew, he was running along the river road, with the girl Ethel astride his shoulders. She held reins to a metal bit in his mouth that was jammed in between his teeth. When Wally woke up, just before dawn, he was in the easy chair in his own house. The door was open. Wally's pants were torn and his legs were scratched.

Wally had crazy thoughts about the night before. Was it true or was it all a dream? Before he could decide, the pow wow man from down river appeared at the door as he oft times did, to buy some eggs. The two men had coffee together and Wally told the old man about the pretty wife of the young blacksmith and the events of the night before. He showed the old man his legs, scratched as if he had indeed travelled through brush and brambles.

The old man was upset. He smoked his pipe and went into deep thought. Then he told Wally that the happenings of the night before could very well be true. Such things had been known to happen. Wally appeared to be coming under the spell of a black witch and the power of the Devil.

The pow wow smoked some more and said some prayers. He took some herbs from two small buckskin amulets on a thong around his neck and made some tea for Wally to drink. Then he told Wally that the girl would probably return that night as the moon was just going past being full.

If the girl returned, when she took Wally's hand, he was to grab her and put a bit in her mouth and a bridle on her. He was to have the bit and bridle with him under his shirt, ready to use. Then the girl, if she was truly a witch would turn into a bridled mare and could be led to a stout stall in the barn and locked up for the night, no matter what kind of a rumpus she raised. Wally told the old man that he'd have to be crazy to believe in such things. The old feller simply puffed on his pipe, with a slight smile on his face, and a twinkle in his dark eyes.

"Drink more of my tea," said the pow wow.

That night, as Wally sat in the big chair and the moon arose, an hour later than the night before, there came the sound of hoofbeats and the girl appeared at his door. She rushed to Wally, threw her arms around him, kissed him and said, "I have someone with me to take my mare back to the Corners. You will come with me tonight, never to return."

But Wally was under the influence of the pow Wwow's herb tea. He grabbed the girl and pushed a bit in her mouth as she opened it in surprise. At the same time he placed a bridle around her head. At once she stamped her feet and neighed like a horse. Before his very eyes, the girl turned into a black-maned mare. Following the instructions of the pow wow, he quickly led the strange creature to a stall in the barn and locked the door. Then there was a frenzy of shrill neighing and kicking of the stout planks on the wall.

As he turned from the stall, he found the pow wow Mman standing in the moonlight at the barn door. The old man told Wally that he had done well and they went in the house to talk over coffee and the smell of the smoke from the old man's pipe. After a while they took a couple of lanterns and went to the barn, to quell the excitement of the other horses that Wally had in the barn. Then they returned to house and to sleep.

The next morning, the pow wow and Wally left the farm for Osborn Bridge in a horse-drawn buggy, the strange black mare at the end of a lead-rope behind them. They went straight to the smitty. There, the pow wow told young Cliff Harris to put a shoe on the left front foot of the black mare, which was unsettled and trying to jerk loose.

Cliff took a hot metal shoe from the red-hot coals of the forge and with his long-handled metal tongs tried to place the shoe against the left front hoof of the black mare. As soon as the red-hot shoe touched the hoof there was a flash of bright light and the mare turned into his black-haired young wife, Ethel. She screamed and pulled loose. Cliff dropped the tongs in horror. Wally and the pow wow rushed to the door and saw the girl running for the river.

Ethel did not return. A search was made and her body was found in the river. And for years it was the talk of the valley. Because, whether the whole story was true or not, there were very reliable people that swore that when they looked at the body of the young woman her hand was burned.

CHASIN' THE DEVIL AT POVERTY HILL

One Sunday morning after services the preacher of Beecher's Hollow Church asked the Widow Glass why she had stopped coming to the Wednesday night prayer meeting.

"I'm afraid to come out my door at night," she said, "especially to walk the road and carry a lantern in the darkness."

The preacher was concerned. Why was she so fearful of the dark?

Her cabin, Widow Glass told him, was surely cursed. There was an evil spirit lurking outside in the dark. There was this moving dark shadow, strange noises that scared her and her cat.

Had she actually seen this strange spirit, if that indeed is what it was, the preacher asked. Maybe it was just a tree branch scraping the roof of the house?

No, Widow Glass said, even though she was too scared to go outside at night she had seen the mark of that spirit. Each morning she saw cloven hoof marks in the soft earth outside her cabin. Surely it was an imp of Satan or the Devil himself after her at night.

The preacher promised to help her. He would hold the next Wednesday Night Prayer Meeting at her home. Prayers would drive the Devil away. Hhe passed the word of the change of the meeting place around to his flock and advised them not to walk alone to the cabin at Poverty Hill. Come by twos and threes and carry lanterns.

Wednesday night, the ladies gathered at the cabin of

Widow Glass. The preacher told them why they were meeting there. That they were going to chase the Devil away with the power of their prayers. They would cleanse this bewitched cabin.

So they had their prayers and sung some hymns. Then a woman said in a scared voice, "I hear footsteps."

The prayers and singing stopped. Other women said that they, too, heard something outside. A woman near the window said she could hear the very breathing of the Devil and could smell brimstone.

Then she and another lady screamed that they could see horns at the window. They were the horns of the Devil coming to catch someone and drag her off to Hades!

The preacher hurried to the window and waved his Good Book. He shouted at the Devil, "Begone!" Then he actually threw his Bible at the window and those horns that could clearly be seen outside.

All the women did likewise and the glass shattered. The horns withdrew from the ray of light shining out the window. They heard a swishing noise and hurried footsteps and then all was quiet.

The preacher opened the door and, coal oil lantern in hand, stepped into the blackness of the night. He heard only the calls of crickets and katy-dids, with the far off lonely cry of an owl. The Devil Beast was gone.

The women also came outdoors with their lanterns. There, in the earth under the window in the midst of the shattered glass and Bibles, were the cloven hoof marks of the Evil One.

So, right outside there by the broken window in the mellow, yellow lite of the lanterns, the good women raised their voices in prayer and song. They had bested the Evil One and made Poverty Hill a safe place to live in again. They all returned home with joy.

Talk quickly went up and down the valley about the

valiant preacher and the brave women of his flock getting the best of Old Nick. The Devil had truly been driven from the valley.

And, the very next morning, Marcus Rowan, neighbor to Widow Glass, finally got around to repairing his pasture fence.

HE WANTED TO LEARN OF WITCHES AND DEMONS

This story I'm gonna tell you is about a writer who came to the valley. He said he wanted to live alone and study about witches and demonology. Then write about them.

Well, true enough, there were some "witch ladies" as they were called. Mostly they were old granny women who helped women who was gonna have a baby, at what was called "birthin' time," and those women were good at it. They were kind, understanding and knowledgeable. Doctors in those days were few with many miles between. Travel was by horse and wagon or buggy, over rough roads in good weather and nigh impossible in bad.

A granny woman would know when a woman's time was comin' and go to her house, cabin or shack, even on snowshoes in winter. She'd plan to stay over several days, taking care of mother, baby and the housework. Also, a granny woman was full of the know-how as to what herbs and roots were needed to treat sickness and injury.

They were women needed in almost any area. Some of the granny women did know other things; they were a sort of mysterious people. Many were psychic, could sort of look into the future. They could tell fortunes in many ways that they'd studied. Know-how was generally passed down from mother to daughter. The granny women or witch women of the valley were mostly with blood from England, Ireland, Scotland and Wales. A few were German. Olga, the witch lady over the mountains, south of the valley in the area of North Green-field, had come over from Central Europe.

Anyway, he bought the old George Morris farm. It was located along the river on the side-hill, east of Batchellerville and west of Conklingville. Near as I could trace the location, it was east of Dailey Creek. Years later it was flooded for the reservoir and camps were built along new roads above the lake. A clubhouse called "Overlook" was built uphill on part of the land. I know of that place, 'cause I played with a hillbilly and square dance band at the Overlook Club.

So, this writer bought the Old Morris Farm, not much more than a fair size clearing chopped out of the wilderness. River down in front, forest on three sides, except for the desolate river road. The road was from Batchellerville to Conklingville. Nothin' along it but a few houses in an eighteen mile stretch of rough dirt road.

That writer, Olin Owens, wanted to be alone. He surely was. He bought a horse and saddle so he could ride east or west to either small town and other places and a boat so he could row across the river to the north side and land near Huntsville, which has since been flooded by the lake waters. He asked folks questions and they, being shy of newcomers didn't have much to say except, "Howdy, nice day," and "Goodbye." So he was a stranger in a strange land. He was alone.

Then his saddle horse got sick. He got in his boat and rowed across the river and asked for an animal doctor. He was told there was no such thing in 40-50 miles. But some person, feeling sorry to hear about a sick horse, told him that there was a witch lady who took care of sick critters and she lived on the same side of the river as he did. Owens, he went by boat to see the lady, told how his horse was sick and offered to pay her for help. Pay. That was the magic word, 'cause those days cash money was hard to come by. Lots of

113

things were done on a barter system, but cash, that was what made the world go round.

With the use of herbs, incantations and burning of black chicken feathers, the witch woman cured the horse. She became friendly with Mister Owens and gave him some information on witches and witchery. She also told him of several witches living in the valley.

One was a male witch, but he wouldn't talk to Olin. In fact, he chased him off his place with a shotgun. Likewise, an old woman would have nothin' to do with the newcomer. But Olin was assured that a young, pretty witch that lived beyond Osborn Bridge would most likely be friendly and talk to him.

Olin had been alone and maybe was feeling lonely. The thought of meeting a pretty young lady was interesting. He saddled his horse, packed a bedroll and rode up river to Osborn Bridge. You must understand there was a covered bridge and also a small village. Both bore the name Osborn Bridge. That whole area was in later years flooded by the waters.

Olin got to meet the young witch lady. Her name was Kate and she lived near the Big Vly, a vast swamp, morass and place of many streams. Kate did talk to him a little. So Olin rented an empty house near the village. He liked Kate.

Alone! That word which had meant so much when he was by himself and free was a word he now hated. All he wanted was to forget he had said it. He wanted, more than anything, to see and talk and be near the girl Kate. There was no longer the beauty of nature to see and enjoy. He cared not for the sun, clouds, stars, sunrise, birds in song, or the moving waters of the river.

He found himself longing for the sight of Kate, the song in her voice, sunlight or lamplight on her hair. She was a walking dream, but she acted as if she hardly knew that he was alive. The water in the river became black to him. He saw no beauty in it, only in Kate. The sky's blue deepened to black, he saw no horizon, he saw only Kate. She had cast a spell and bewitched him.

The storekeep told him, as a friend, to forget Kate, and return home, down river. Many local people believed that Kate could be dangerous to men who fell for her charms. At night, Olin could no longer sleep, only toss and turn. Then, one night, Kate appeared to him in a dream. She kissed him and then turned him into a horse. She placed his own saddle on his back, mounted and rode him. The young witch who had become his one desire rode him as a horse along the country roads, along the river and the more solid grounds of the marshland of Big Vly. When he was near exhausted, she rode him back to his rented house, removed the saddle, gave him a kiss and left. As he entered the door he changed into his own self, fell into bed and a deep sleep.

In the morn he awoke, stiff and sore with cuts and bruises on his legs and body. He heated some coffee, drank it and went to the store. The storekeep took one look at him, then took him to a room behind the store and placed him on a small bed there while sending a small boy to fetch the preacher.

The preacher man came, looked at Olin Owens and asked him some questions. As soon as he learned about the dream, the man of the cloth shook his head. Olin, he was on dangerous ground. He must see no more of Kate. He must saddle his horse at once and ride down river.

"Otherwise," said the preacher, "You are doomed. She pleasures herself with you. You are under the power of a demon, a succubus that takes the form of a woman, goes to a man at night, possesses him and changes him. You must leave here! Leave before the shadows grow long, when the sun starts to set in the west. Should the shadows reach you, you cannot escape with your soul. Flee, young man, flee! Forget this bad moment in your life, this creature, or the night to come may well be your last."

That is just what the preacher said. So I was told by the grandson of the preacher.

The storekeep and the preacher had a man saddle the horse. They put the reins in Olin's hands and started him down river. But the next morning the horse was found, saddled and grazing along the river. The area was searched but the rider was not found. The local constable had a search made in the river. No results. The State Police were called in, also with no results. Downriver at the farm of Olin Owens there was no sign of him. His possessions were still there.

When Kate was told by the constable about the missing man, she is reported to have laughed and said, "Well, he wanted to learn of witches and demons. Do you suppose he did?"

WOLF MAN

Walter was a strange man and had been a strange boy growing up. He was named Walter at birthing time. No one ever got friendly enough to call him Walt, Wal, Wally, or any such. He became known as Black Walter.

As a boy he'd act like he was some kind of monster. He'd not only chase kids at school but grab 'em and even bite 'em, saying he wanted to drink of their blood. He'd growl like a dog or a wolf. Other kids stayed away from him as far as they could. Once he set fire to the school house, another time the church. Both times his parents paid money to get things fixed and not have their Walter sent away, as some folks wanted done.

Then a farmer caught him at his barn cutting the tail off his horse. That farmer beat that boy within an inch of his life. Picked him up and carted him home in his horse and buggy. Carried him up and just dumped him on the porch floor like a sack of potatoes. A neighbor heard the farmer call out to Walter's parents, "Come out and get your whelp of Satan! The likes of him don't belong in Heaven and I doubt if even Lucifer will want him in Hell!"

As Walter grew older he got smarter and slyer. He did things but folks just couldn't prove it was him as did it. Like someone caught Missus Sims' cat, put coal oil on it, set the poor animal on fire. Scared like, it ran for home and under the barn. Barn burned down with four cows and a winter's supply of hay in it. State Police was called in but there was no proof.

Another time Mister Marten's cows got sick, some

117

died. An animal doctor was brought in all the way from over at Fonda. He decided it was poison. The hay in the barn had been dusted with Paris Green. Arsenic. It was used those days by many folk to spray or dust the potato vines growing in the fields, to kill bugs. Again no proof. Black Walter laughed and said he didn't do it.

Sheep was killed. Goats, dogs and any kind of small animal or bird you could think of. Some small animals were skinned and the bare bloody carcasses tied to an outside door knob of a house. In the dark a few knocks came on the door. The farmer or house person would go to answer the door. No one was there. If they stepped out on the porch to make sure and found nobody, they would then reach for the doorknob to go back in and grasp the bloody body tied there. It was a terrible scare, especially for women folk and enough to stop the heart of many a man. By then folks was callin' the boy Black Walter for the black deeds he done. Next he was caught with a tied-up little girl. He had really bitten her like a savage animal. He was sent away for that deal.

Some years later the word went up the valley. "Walter is back!"

Soon things began to happen. But there was no proof. A couple of men said in the store that enough of them should get together and hang Black Walter some night. But it was just talk. They weren't mean enough to do such a thing. But it needed doin'.

Walter began to wear a big, long fur coat, made of wolf skins. He snarled and growled at folks more than ever. Some said that he was a raving monster full of madness and vengefulness.

One night there was gunfire at a sheepfold. When it was checked out, several sheep were found dead in the snow. A set of human footprints led to the sheep fold. There were empty rifle shells at the fence of the fold, a rifle in the snow and the big wolfskin fur coat of Walter—but there was no Walter and no tracks in the snow showing he had walked away. A search was made, fearing some sort of trick to cause further trouble. Nothing!

The State Police, the men in gray with the big hats, came and looked everything over, talked to folks. They finally put it down as a simple disappearance. Walter was never seen again. It was believed by many that the Devil had finally come claimed his own. The wolfskin coat was nailed, spread out, to the side of the barn by some local fellers like an animal skin.

I've often wondered what happened that winter night when the footprints stopped in the snow. Who knows?

THE WITCH OF MAD DOG HILL

The Great Sacandaga Lake was formed when a dam was built and the gates were closed in 19 and 30. The waters made a lake 29 miles long and as wide in some places as 5 miles. The surface area of 42 square miles covers among other things some strange happenings and stories.

I'd like to tell you a strange story of a witch. This story was told to me sixty or so years ago.

Winter had started in the valley. There was a horse and wagon on the rough dirt road that led to Huntsville. On the wagon were two men. They were going to a remote farm to meet a man there and complete the purchase of a large tract of timberland on one of the mountains above the valley. They had gotten a late start and now the short day was drawing to a close. Snow was falling and there was very little visibility. So they began to look for a shelter for the night and food for themselves and their horse, away from the storm.

Dwellings were few and far apart. They were really worried. Finally they saw a dim light ahead in the darkness. As they got close they saw it came from a window in a small house near the road. There was also a barn and they drove their horse there—as was the custom—unhitched it from the wagon, led it in the barn to a stall and gave it some hay.

Going to the house they knocked on the door which was opened by an old lady. She told the travellers to enter. They asked to stay the night and for some food. The lady said, "Yes."

They handed her some money from a bag they carried.

The lady told them to remove their wet coats and boots and place them near the hearth of an open fireplace where there was a cheery fire burning. There were three large dogs near the fireplace; the lady told them to move and they did. Then the lady told the travelers to be seated on a bench at the table and she handed each one a chunk of cornbread and a bowl of hot stew. They told the next day that the lady said it was goat meat, potatoes, onions and herbs in a thick broth. She gave them native chickory to drink.

After the fine meal, she handed each man a blanket and told them that they could sleep on the floor by the fireplace, the dogs across from them. She herself had a bed in a small room adjoining. She had told them that her name was Granny Holly Cale. Her man Cal Cale had lost his life in the river years ago. She put out the flame in the coal oil lamp and all was quiet.

The men slept well after their trip and the food. John woke up at dawn; the fire had burned down to a bed of red coals. John went to stretch, raising his arms and was shocked to see hairy paws sticking out of his shirt sleeves. He touched his face. It was covered with hair too! His nose was strange and long. John gave out a loud yell, but the noise came out a yelp!

An answering yelp next to him was his friend and business partner Henry. John looked—now there were four dogs on the floor by the fireplace. One of them had on the clothes of Henry, but the face of a dog.

John and Henry, both scared, looked at one another. They had dog-like heads but human brains and eyes. It was not possible. It was incredible, unbelievable, it was crazy, but somehow the old lady, a witch, had turned them into dogs.

They looked at one another, then at the door. John tried to stand erect but found himself on hands and feet on all fours on the floor. Doglike, four feet. As he scrambled around one of his feet knocked over the pile of wood at the fireplace. The other man dog Henry was getting himself together also. The other three dogs just looked at them with strange eyes.

The two got to the door and jiggled the latch. Fortunately there was no door knob. The door swung outward. When they got through the door, Henry pulled the latch string with his teeth and pushed the door shut. John and Henry somehow pushed a large bench on the porch in front of the door—to slow down any pursuit was in their minds. Then, on all fours, like dogs they ran to the road. It had stopped snowing as they ran down the snow covered road away from the terrible house, the crazy old woman and the three large dogs in it. Their running in such a manner tore their clothes. They kept running and running as if the old lady, the dogs and the Devil himself were all at their heels.

Then, suddenly, they saw a man walking toward them in the road. They stopped, then went toward the man. He started shouting and waving a heavy walking stick at them, thinking they were two dogs after him. He swung the walking stick and as he did sunlight flashed on a silver cross on the head of the walking stick.

The dogs stopped. Then, instead of two large dogs the startled man saw two men crouched in the snow. The two men were scared, barefoot in the snow. The man was a local preacher, taking a morning walk in the fresh snow. The two travellers found now that they had returned to human form they could stand erect and talk. The preacher thought they were strange but told them he wanted to get them out of the snow and cold.

He took them to his house, next to a small church. He and his wife warmed, fed and clothed the two men and listened to their story. The preacher said some local people believed that Granny Holly Cale was a witch

124

and there was talk to that effect about her. But it was only such things as cows that didn't give milk or hens with no eggs and such whispers. He never took any stock in it.

The preacher took John and Henry to see the local constable who listened to the story. He gathered some men and they headed for Mad Dog Hill to see what was going on. The preacher stuck to his story that he first thought the two were fierce dogs charging at him when he waved his walking stick, the clothes were from some previous victim. Then they changed into humans. He still thought they'd had a drinking party or some wild nightmare together. He still couldn't believe the woman could have changed them into dogs. Nor could the constable and men.

But then they reached the spot where the footprints of the preacher, and the mark in the snow of his cane, met the sets of tracks coming down the road. A very close examination of all prints was made. There were the tracks of two dogs, coming through the snow. Where they met the preacher they became changed into shoeless human feet.

Soon they came to where they could see the barn, but the house was no longer there. It had burned to the ground, wisps of smoke still rising upward.

They searched the ruins and all around. They hitched the horse to the wagon and in the wagon they placed a burlap bag with what they figured was the skull and some bones of the witch. In another bag they placed three dog skulls and some bones. The lumbermen's bag with the money in it was gone.

One of the old timers in the group remembered that years before there had been a log cabin that burned to the ground at that spot. This house had been built right on the old site as it was near a spring. He also told that at the time of the fire, there had been a mad dog running around that was shot and buried. They returned to Huntsville.

A story? Yes! But one of those two lumbermen lost three toes and the other chap lost a frozen ear! That part was real. For this story was told me by the great-grandson of the traveller who lost his ear to frost that time in the Valley.

Now the lake waters cover Huntsville and "Mad Dog Hill!"

PART FOUR:

A GHOST IS NEVER SEEN WITHOUT MITTENS

BEAR TOOTH BRADY'S CHOPPERS

Watson Brady was given the nickname "Beartooth" because he, a well-to-do lumberman and sawmill owner, was attacked by a bear, lost his teeth and had to get a set of dentures made.

The story was that Watson had his teamster drive him and a load of supplies to his number two lumber camp on Catamont Hill. Being Sunday all the men at camp had the day off. Even the cook.

The team and wagon pulled into the camp clearing. Watson told the teamster to start unloading at the supply shed while he went to the cook shack to see how things were.

The door of the cook shack was closed. Watson pulled the latch string. The door swung inward and as Watson stepped in, he found himself facing a big black bear that had gotten in the building by smashing a rear window. The bear had smashed cans of beans, jars of honey and eaten a ham and side of bacon. As the door opened, the bear headed for the opening, taking a swipe at Watson and knocking him to the floor. The teamster saw the bear leave the shack. He found his boss man unconscious on the floor, his face a bloody mess.

The man got Watson into the wagon and drove down to the river, across the covered bridge to Batchlerville to the doctor that was there at that time. The doc patched up Watson's face as well as he could sent him on to the hospital at Gloversville. After a time Watson Brady recovered. His broken jaw had been wired

up. Most of his teeth had been smashed out so they had a set of uppers and lowers made and fitted in his mouth. That's how come he got the nickname Beartooth Brady tagged on him.

Watson Brady had always been a stern, mean man. But after the accident and becoming named Beartooth he really took it out on his missus. They said Missus Brady was a real nice woman that married the wrong man. But now she really went through hell with Beartooth. He grew more mean, grumpy and bitter, especially because the trouble with the bear had cost him so much money. These were the days before there was much insurance coverage. He had none and had to pay out cash money. Missus Brady told someone that she had married Watson for better or worse and he'd gotten worse for sure.

But Watson was mighty proud of those false teeth, "choppers" he called them. He used to take them out of his head, show them to strangers and tell, as he told it, about the bear fight that he'd had at Camp Number Two up on Catamont Hill. In his telling of the happening, he had licked the bear. Every night Beartooth took out his choppers and put them in a cup on a bedside table. That was to rest his jaws.

One day, somehow, Beartooth fell or slipped into the whirling saw blade at the sawmill. That finished Beartooth Brady. All but his teeth. It seems that morning he hadn't put his teeth back in his head because his mouth hurt. After the funeral Missus Brady found the teeth on the bedside table. In the excitement, and what with the horrible mangling the saw did to Beartooth, and those being the days before embalming, Beartooth had just been scooped up, put in a box which was then nailed shut and buried next morn, at Shady Rest Buryin' Ground.

Well, Missus Brady looked at those choppers and kept them as a macabre memory that Beartooth was

131

gone. She showed them to some lady friends and said she knew he wouldn't be needing them as he must have gone to Hell to join Old Nick.

However, those teeth on the bedside table began to bother the woman, for they'd rattle around in the dark as if the spirit of Beartooth had come back and was fumbling around for his teeth. Beartooth Brady's false teeth rattled and clapped and snapped most every night. Finally, one night, the choppers jumped off the table and bit the woman! They chewed on her like a mad dog. She ran out of the house screaming.

She was bleeding and gashed when a neighbor found her and took her to the constable. When the officer came to the house, those false teeth were sitting there on the floor as innocent as could be, even though there was blood on them. The constable took them out to a tree stump in the yard and busted them with an axe.

That was the last of Beartooth Brady!

THE HOUSE ON SPOOKY KNOLL

They said the house on Richards Knoll, called Spooky Hill, had a haint into it.

Two or three or so families had moved in and moved out. Much the same stories were told by each. Even with the cupboard closed the plates and cups would become broken. There was a drawer for such table stuff as knives, forks and spoons. These would be heard to rattle around. Then, with not a person touching it, the drawer would slide out of its place onto the floor and scatter the table stuff. Once in a while one or two forks and spoons would be bent and twisted as i fa pair of strong hands had done it.

You couldn't leave a lamp or a lantern lit in a room unless some real person was right close to it. Otherwise the flame might just blow out in that closed room, or worse yet, get somehow thrown to the floor where the spilled oil would start a fire. That happened at least twice but the fires got caught in time and put out by smothering them with something. Two of the rooms had burnt places on the floor and one had a scorched wall.

Every now and then some small item would just go sailing across a room to smash against the furniture or a wall or, every now and then, a person. They couldn't keep the shades up on the windows. If pulled down at eventide they'd soon be loose, roll up on the roller real quick like and give a snap. Or they'd come off the window in a rumpled mess like some mad person pulled them down and threw them in a heap.

133

Doors would slam bang. Prop a window up to get some fresh valley air and like as not the prop would fall out and the window smash down, sometimes smashing a window light. Or a smokey looking sort of a figure would wander through the rooms, passing through closed doors and even the walls.

Once a lady in a sunbonnet came up on the porch and sat in a chair next to the current lady of the house, who started to talk to the visitor, thinking she was a neighbor woman come to talk to her so she bid her welcome. But when she looked a little closer, lo and behold, she could see right through the visitor! The lady of the house flung aside the pan of peas she was shelling and went running to her husband in the barn.

He grabbed a pitchfork and ran for the house, not thinking of how he was going to prod a ghost with the tines of his fork. Of course there was no one, nothing there. He searched the house. The dwelling sat on that there open knoll and had there been anyone or anything a leavin', he'd a sure enough seen it.

That feller ran back the barn, hitched the team to the wagon and he and his Missus loaded up their belongings and headed for Hadley Town way down the river. They never went back to the house on the knoll.

Of course, word spread around about the latest doin's at the house on Spooky Knoll. No use my goin' through what happened to the other couple families that tried livin' in the house. Much the same sort of doin's, you understand.

With the word goin' round about the latest doin's at the house on the knoll, a feller by name of Dick Talbot, a French Canadian and Injun kind of a feller, he got interested. This here Dick Talbot, I mind it's down on the records somewheres, that he was a barber, tooth puller, carpenter and undertaker. Made coffins and fixed bodies for buryin'. He was in Conklingville, which those days as I was told, had a slew of houses, church, school, general store, woodmaking mill, a tannery and such like.

This here barber, him being part Injun, he knew a thing or two or three. He was called a pow wow doctor. He went out in the woods, got some wild herbs, cut some chips from some trees, cooked up all that stuff and went to the house on the knoll. He poured his herb mixture down the open well, which was stoned up, burned some other herbs in the house, said some prayers and after that, I was told, there was no more spooks!

THE STAINED
GRAVE STONE

There was the story I heard of the tombstone in the buryin' ground at Beecher's Hollow. The stone bled at a certain time each year.

Years before a man was in an awful accident when his team of horses got spooked and ran away. It was decided that he was dead and they buried him, that hot summer day, in the graveyard next the church.

That was before the days of the embalming of a body. His wife had a stone put at the grave. A little more than a year after the poor man was buried a red stain appeared on a top corner of his gravestone. The stain was small at first. Then it began to grow and ooze a liquid, a red liquid. People called it blood. The preacher had a man try to remove the stain, but all he could do was to stop the oozing—or bleeding as folks now called it.

Some folks claimed that the man really wasn't dead when they buried him and that was why the stone bled. They said the poor feller had come to and tried to scratch his way out of the pine box that he found himself in. They said he broke his fingernails and wore his fingers to the bone trying to dig his way out of the enclosing earth. But he had finally bled to death.

A nearby witch woman who lived at Skull Hill made it known that the stone was the sign of a tormented spirit that couldn't rest. That spirit caused the stone to bleed to show his upset. That stone would show blood every year on the day he really died when he was in the ground. She tried several times in different ways to put the lost soul at rest. But she failed. The stone remained stained and I was told that the stain was renewed every year.

Now I don't claim that the story was true. But one of the fellers that worked in the Boneyard Gang, which dug up and removed the remains of hundreds of folks, putting them to final rest at Union Mills and Vail Mills above the flood waters, told me there really was an old cracked, weathered headstone that had a dark stain on it.

But what? Was it a sort of fungus or a mildew—or was it really blood stains?

THE TALKING SPIRIT

There was a man, wife and little boy riding in an open buggy up the river road. It was raining. They came to a log cabin and the man reined the horse into the barn lot. It was the custom in those days, that if you needed a night's lodging you were welcome to just about any house you came to and your horse to the barn. The family would put you up for the night and provide supper and breakfast. If you could pay something, fine. If you couldn't you were still welcome. It was a nice custom in the valley.

The man unhitched the horse and put it in a stall in the barn and wife and boy went to the house. There was no one at home, the door unlocked. The mother took the boy into the kitchen, found a lamp and lit it on the table. All the while she kept calling out that she was there and asking if anyone was at home. She thought possibly everyone was asleep. But there was no one in the cabin.

The man finished at the barn and came into the house. He started a fire in the kitchen fireplace, went out to the woodshed, got more wood and went to the wagon and got food from a box they carried. He took that and some blankets to the cabin. The woman saw a bucket and a path into the woods and got some water from a spring.

There was furniture in the cabin but everything was covered with dust as if no one had been there for awhile. The lady dusted things off and scrubbed the kitchen table and some chairs. Then she took a pot of cooked beans from the box her husband had brought from the wagon and put the beans at the fire to warm up. They ate beans, dry corn bread and washed it down with spring water. It was still raining outdoors, but they were dry and warm.

The man and lady went into a bedroom next to the kitchen, dusted off a couple of corn shuck mattresses and shook them up. The man and boy went to bed, just taking off their shoes. The woman decided to sit up awhile in the kitchen at the table where the lamp gave her light to read from the small Bible she took from her reticule. As she sat reading in the lamp light a drop of red liquid fell from a loft overhead, fell right on the page she was reading. She touched it with a finger thinking it might be some sort of a pine pitch that had oozed from a log rafter overhead.

But it wasn't sticky nor did it smell of pitch. Then another drop fell on the page. She took her kerchief and wiped it off. It seemed like blood to her and that scared her because she thought perhaps an injured bird, or worse and animal was up in the loft above her.

She rose from her chair to go to her husband in the bedroom, but then she saw the man sitting on the edge of the loft. In the lamplite she saw the raw, red gash on his neck.

"Don't be afraid," the man said. "You're the only person not to scream and flee when I came back. Please, wait . . ."

The woman, thinking he was truly just an injured man, asked could she help the awful cut on his neck?

"No one can help me," the apparition answered, "for I am not of your world. I cannot rest until my bones are buried." Then he told her where his bones were hidden, there under the floor. If she would bury them by the apple tree, she could have his money that was concealed nearby, underneath a stone. Two men had killed him but they did not find the money. That money would be hers. Then he faded from sight.

140

The woman hurried to the bedroom and wakened her husband. He and she sat at the table as she showed him the red marks on the Bible page and told the story. He was amazed but he knew his wife was truthful, level-headed and religious. He believed her.

The next morning the man tore up some of the boards of the loft floor and found a skeleton. They hitched their horse to the wagon and, taking the boy, drove on to Huntsville. There they told the story to the constable and a preacher man. Those two and some other men from the store went with the man, wife and boy, back to the farm. The murdered man's bones were buried under the apple tree and the man of cloth said a prayer. Nearby, the money was found hidden under that stone. There was no kin so the constable gave the gold and silver coins to the couple.

THE GRAVE TREE

She was a pretty girl. One of the most pretty in that part of the valley, it was said. She was called Little Nance. As sometimes happened, she gave her love to a well-to-do married man. She became great with child and folks scorned her. As her time approached, Little Nance became very sad and depressed. And so the body of that poor girl, no more than a child herself, was found hanging from a limb in a big beech tree one summer day.

A couple of men hastily made a coffin, a pine box from some boards. In those days in the remote valley a body was buried quickly as there was no embalming. But where to bury the poor child? The preacher at Osborn Bridge forbade the burial of a suicide in his church yard buryin' ground. Her only kin was an uncle who was working in another state. So, the body of Little Nance was buried in a grave under the big beech tree where she spent her last moments of life.

Talk in the area about the happening quieted down. But, one night, the man who owned a sawmill and had been whispered about as having been the lover of the dead girl had an unpleasant dream. He awoke screaming. His wife had a time getting him to calm down.

This happened several nights in a row. The mill owner got so he was scared to go to bed, but sat up drinking. Finally, with his nerves all shot, he confessed that the ghost of Little Nance had been appearing most every night.

The spirit held out her arms to him, he said, beckoning for him to follow her. He was finally taken over to

Gloversville to have a doctor see him. The doctor just gave him some medication and sent the man home.

Then the missing uncle of the dead girl returned. Of course, he was shocked when he learned of her tragic death and where she was buried. He was told of the nightmares of the mill owner. The uncle went to both the preacher and the sawmill man, asking that his neice be put to rest properly, but he received no satisfaction.

At last, someone told him about witch that lived in the castle near Big Vly. He went to see her and related the sad story. The witch, of course, had heard the gossip. After he crossed her palm with silver, as was the custom, she told him the spirit of his niece was in torment and could not rest. By the way the spirit appeared, beckoning to the sawmill man, he was being urged to follow and learn something.

The witch lady got a piece of the man's clothing off his family clothes line. With that she was able to cast a spell on the man. The next night, when the dead girl's ghost appeared at his home, the man followed her spirit to the big beech tree. There he flung himself on the grave and began to dig in the dust with his bare hands.

The witch and the uncle had followed at a distance and saw this. The next morning the witch hired two strong men to dig up the girl's pine box coffin. In the coffin they found the body of Little Nance and right beside her the body of a tiny baby girl. The uncle went to the constable and the preacher and demanded that both bodies be given a decent Christian burial in the church graveyard. This was done.

Then the witch and the uncle went to the sawmill. There they learned that when the constable told the sawmill man the story of the two bodies in that grave, the man ran and threw himself into the big saw that ripped boards from the logs. The sawmill man died at once.

For many years after that, people called that big beech "The Grave Tree!"

143

TWO GRAVE MARKERS

I heard a story about a witch who lived along the desolate part of the river, the part called South Side by some folks. It was between the mouth of Dailey Creek and the part of Conklingville that was across the river. At one time Conklingville had houses and mills on both sides of the river. There was a Conklingville bridge and down stream there was the Stewart's Bridge.

Well, the husband of this witch had been killed by a falling tree in the lumber woods. The widow mourned the man's death so much that she got another witch from upriver to come see her. The next full moon the two witch ladies held some sort of witchery ceremony. Through their magic they caused the dead man to be reborn from the afterworld. However, the reborn man was not right in the head from the injury of the falling tree. A few nights after the full moon his body was found hanging by a rope from a tree limb in the apple orchard.

So he was buried, same as the first time, across the river in the Huntsville Buryin' Ground. It was said he was buried alongside the first of his graves. There were two head boards, side by each, with the same man's name on them!

So, curious me, I asked why they hadn't opened up the first grave to see what was in it?

"That would have been sacrilegious," I was told.

THE HAND

The lumber merchant reached Beecher's Hollow and asked at a farm house if he could buy supper and lodging for the night for he and his horse. He was served a meal but was told the house was full as several other travellers had put in before him. However, they'd give him a blanket and he could sleep in the barn on some hay near his horse.

He turned in early, first putting a pouch of money under some hay he used for a pillow. He slept well at first but the next thing he knew he was half awake, gasping for breath. Something was pressing hard on his windpipe shutting off the air. He thought it was a thief after his money, reached for his gun but failed to find it in the darkness.

Whatever it was tightened the grip on Whelan's throat. At first, he thought that it was a snake at his throat because of the way it felt—all cold and clammy. Then, as he grabbed at it, he realized it was a wrist. He felt for the body. There was none. Just the cold hand and wrist at his throat!. Finally, he wrenched the hand from his throat and arose. He struck a match. As far as he could tell there was only his own horse and two others in the stalls.

Both barn doors were closed, just as they had been when he settled down in the hay. His money bag was there and he found his gun. He thought he was growing crazy or he'd had a wild nightmare. Finally he settled down in the hay and fell asleep. The next morning he went to the house and related his story, expecting to be laughed at.

145

Instead, he was told that this had happened before. Many years ago a man lost his hand in an axe fight at the place directly at the place under where the barn had been built. The belief was that every now and then the man's spirit returned. Seeking revenge, the lost hand would materialize and attack whoever was in the barn. Whelan said they were all crazy and through some trick had tried to steal his money.

"Hand be damned," he said.

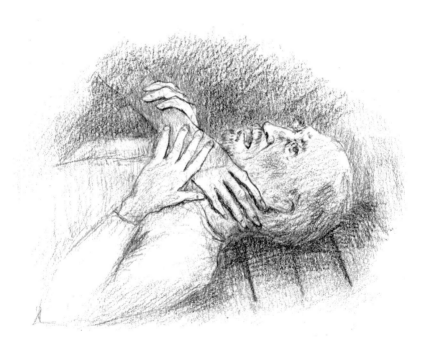

HALF A DOZEN
COFFIN NAILS

The story as I got it was that Dean Gavin was crossing the river in a canoe from his farm at Big Thumb. One of those sudden storms of the valley roared down the river, the wind and waves overturned the canoe. Dean drowned.

A fisherman huddled under a tree saw the body in Black Eddy and pulled it on shore. He ran for help, which came. They drained the water from the body but Dean did not regain life. He was buried in the church yard at Croweville. People consoled the widow.

That night Missus Gavin had a dream that Dean had turned over in his coffin and seemed to be struggling to escape. She woke up screaming, waking her sister who had stayed with her for the night. Missus Gavin insisted the dream was true and was all for having the grave opened up right then in the middle of the night. Her sister told her they could do nothing then, to wait for morning. She got her to drink some coffee and back to bed.

After a while, the poor woman had the same dream and woke up screaming. By the time the sister got her calmed down it was daybreak. The sister said it was a nightmare and got some more coffee into the widow. As soon as the sun was up enough they dressed and went up to the store and told the story. Someone went and fetched the constable who lived out of town. He listened to the story and then told them it couldn't be so. He also told them that the preacher would not re-

turn again until Sunday services and he was the only one could say to open up a grave in his buryin' ground.

The constable said he himself couldn't figure to open a grave because of a dream. He figured the dream was caused by the emotional strain Missus Gavin had undergone and that digging up the body would only renew the agony and might hurt her mind.

So the two ladies went back to the Gavin home, the widow crying all the time. In about an hour a horse and buggy came up the lane to the house. A witch lady they both knew got out of the buggy, hitched the horse to the porch railing and came to the door. The sister let her in and served coffee.

The witch said she was sorry for Missus Gavin. She'd been to the store and heard about the dream. Then she questioned Missus Gavin and agreed that some dreams were true. The grave should be opened up if only to put the mind of the widow to rest—or possibly help the dead Dean Gavin. After some talk, and the giving of a gift of some silver coins, it was agreed that the widow and sister were to be at the graveyard at dark and to tell no one. The witch would come, bringing two strong men to open the grave and the pine box. If everything was as it should be, they would replace everything, say a prayer and good night. However, if the dream was based on an unknown force, they would take the body, by team and wagon—which they would have—to a man that could possibly help. The witch did not give the man's name at that time.

So, after dark, by the light of a coal oil lantern that swayed from the limb of a tree, the two men dug open the grave, got the box out and pried open the lid. There in the dull lantern light they say that Dean Gavin's body was not on his back as buried, but was twisted to one side with his hands were up in front of his face. There was no sign of life. The widow almost went crazy, but the witch women told the men to put the coffin box and body in the wagon and drive down river road as fast as they could to Conklingville. The three ladies followed in the buggy.

At Conklinville they went to the home of the man who was barber, carpenter, undertaker and a pow wow doctor. He was expecting them as the witch had sent word to him in the afternoon. The pine coffin was carried into his shop, lamps were lit, and curtains were hung to cover the windows. The body was removed from the box and placed on a work bench. In those days in the remote valley there was no embalming. If you died, you were buried!

The witch made three plasters of some kind, tied one on the bottom of each bare foot and strapped a large plaster on the chest of the dead man. It was explained to me that such plasters for a man were to be made by a woman and applied by her. In the case of a woman being dead, a man made and applied the plasters. At the same time the pow wow doctor was saying such prayers as "I know my Redeemer liveth and he will call me from the grave." (I think I remember that correctly.) Pow wow cures were a lot of prayers and strange-sounding words.

The pow wow also heated some bags of salt and placed them under the dead man's arms. He and the witch worked on the dead man. The widow and sister could only stand aside and hope and pray. After a while there was the flicker of an eyelid, then the other one. The body gave a sort of shudder, a gasp and then the man was given some strong grog. (Grog was watered brandy.) In a few minutes there was no doubt that the man was breathing and was alive. The wife was all excited, laughing and crying.

The man was wrapped in wool blankets and heated stones were placed in flannel and placed at his feet. He stirred, then went into a peaceful sleep. The two men left with the team. The pow wow Doctor was paid and went off to bed, leaving the witch and the two sisters sitting around the glow of the fireplace.

I was told that Dean Gavin lived into his eighties. His most treasured possession were half a dozen nails from his own coffin!

IT'S THE DEVIL

The farm on Greenbriar Lane near Sand Creek was a well-cared-for, prosperous-looking place. The owner was not only a farmer, he also owned a grist mill with a water-powered, overshot wheel, that turned some gears that turned the mill stones, that ground the grain for local farmers. The farm and mill owner also had a young wife. Her name was Patrina, one of the loveliest girls in the valley.

Patrina had outward beauty but her heart was evil. She had thoughts of death for her older husband, so that she and her lover might be together forever. She had even told a couple of her lady friends. Patrina would meet her lover at night in the family buryin' place on the farm that had been in her husband's family from the time of the first settlers. Her lover was a common sawmill hand from a nearby creek. He loved Patrina but was content to have things go along as they were, no responsibility.

Patrina's mind became crowded with the death of her husband. She went to see one of the witch women of the valley. The old woman was called a "Black witch", because it was believed she could cast spells and put curses on people. Patrina paid the witch woman a goodly sum of money to cast a spell of death on her husband. She took the witch, as instructed, several swatches of her husbands clothing. She also took three hairs from her husband, her lover and herself.

The witch took the nine hairs, folded them into a small piece of paper, gave the little packet back to the woman and told her to put it under the husband's head, under the mattress. The witch said some incantations. She then told the woman that one of the three owners of those nine hair would soon die a sudden death!

The wife was supposed to meet her lover in the little private farm cemetery a very quiet place, the next Friday night. On Friday afternoon two half-grown neighbor boys caught a couple of the farmer-miller's young shoats running in a back field. The boys knew that they were actually stealing the pigs. In those days, pigs were allowed to run loose and live on natural wild food of roots, nuts and berries. All pigs had notched ears as markers of ownership.

But the boys put the captured pigs in two gunnysacks and decided to hide them among the gravestones in the farm buryin' ground, as it was a nice quiet place. Then they'd return at night and carry them away to hide in a hidden pig sty on an old, empty farm.

So, Friday evening came and the Patrina sneaked off and met her lover. As they settled down on the grass among the gravestones, they were laughing and talking. Probably their voices aroused the two pigs which had gone to sleep in their sacks, as darkness settled on the land. Whatever it was, the two pigs began to kick and thrash and bump around in their sacks and scream, making an awful uproar. You know what I mean if you ever heard two excited pigs. They sure can squeal.

The loving couple were scared by all the noise in the graveyard. The young fella jumped to his feet and yelled, "What in tarnation is all that ruckus?"

"It's the Devil!" screamed Patrina. "The Devil is after me 'cause I wished to kill Harry!" She jumped to her feet and, in her fear and excitement, tripped and fell. Her head hit an old tombstone and she was dead—one of the three as the witch had predicted.

Her lover went to her and when she did not speak to

him, he sat on the ground. He cradled her body in his arms and sat moaning and rocking his lost love! A hired man on the farm heard the squealing of the pigs, and went to the graveyard to investigate. He found the sad sight!

DID THE DEVIL
GET BLACK PETE?

Black Pete drank a lot and mistreated his missus and kids. Finally a granny woman told him that the Devil would be after him for his sins unless he changed his ways.

Pete had been scared of the Devil since he was a little lad. Now with the woman warning him about the Devil he did try to change a little. He wore a hand-carved cross on a rawhide thong around his neck. Even went to far as to carry another such cross in his pocket. Also, he carved crosses in the wood frames over the doors of house and barn.

It was a bad night when Pete left the grog shop. A wild night. The wind howled malevolently and the rain beat against the windows in great gusts. One of the local jokers called out to Pete, "Watch out Pete, this is kind of night the Devil picks to roam the valley."

Black Pete staggered toward home at Bad Water Rapid, but he never got there. He staggered along and off the wet road into some thick brush. He fell down and in falling the chain with the cross around his neck caught on a stub of a thick branch. The ground was slippery. In his drunken state he could not regain his footing. The chain choked him. He was found dead the next morning.

Folks believed that the Devil got him.

SCRATCHING
ON THE CAR ROOF

Greg was the son of a sawmill owner at Shin Bones Creek. The young feller bought one of those new T-Model Fords over to Glens Falls or some such place out of the valley. The events happened on a Saturday night. Greg had driven his girl Liza to a candy-pulling party at the home of her girl friend way out in the country.

On the way home the car ran out of gasoline. Greg had forgotten to fill the extra five gallon can he had in the car. In those days there was only one or two stores in the whole valley that had put in a gas pump out next the hitching rail. There was no electric, so a gas pump to be operational had to be pumped by hand from the underground storage tank up to a gas container on top of the pump. Then it was run through the hose into the car gas tank. Those few folks that owned a car had to also have an extra tank or two to carry gas if they went anywhere so that they would have enough to get home.

Liza told Greg she'd stay in the car and take a nap while Greg went looking for someone who had a horse to lend him to tow the car through the dark woods. Liza fell asleep and woke up only once in the night when she heard scratching on the roof of the car. She told later that she thought it was an owl or some night bird. She had no watch, it was very dark, she had no idea of the time and thought Greg had just left and she had dozed off. So the girl went back to sleep.

Later she was roused from sleep to see it was getting daylight. A strange man was standing next to the car and knocking on the glass with his fist. He was a big rough-looking feller and at first she was scared. The man told her not to be frightened. He was trying to help her. She calmed down, knowing if he meant harm he could have done it as she slept.

The man told her to get out of the car, walk with him and not to look back at the car. However, as she walked with him in the direction he pointed, curiosity got the better of her and she did look back. She screamed and fainted at once. The strange man picked Liza up in his arms and carried her down the road to a farm house where there was a man whose wife and grown daughter could take care of poor Liza.

The strange man was a lumberjack walking home from visiting. He had come upon the T-Model Ford with the girl asleep inside. He and the farmer hitched up the farm horse to a wagon and started off to look for the constable, leaving Liza with the farmer's wife and daughter.

What was it that Liza saw when she disregarded the words of the man to not look back? She saw her boyfriend Greg, hanging by his feet from an overhanging tree limb. His clothes were torn and a rag was around his mouth. He'd had his stomach slit and blood was all over. The constable figured later that when Liza heard scratching on the car roof, it was the fingernails of Greg. One of his hands that he'd worked free just reached down that far.

Swamp Angels were suspected of the crime but it was never proven. The reason? Petty theft and just plain badness in the ones that did the terrible deed. Fortunately they didn't see the girl asleep in the car.

Another tragedy in the valley or a tall tale? I never knew.

157

THE HAT IN THE TAVERN
OR DEAD MAN'S SANDS

First known in the valley as "grog shops," the places began to be known as taverns. They were still much the same. A bar, back bar, foot rail, some spittoons, tables, chairs and always the drinking. Also there were bar room jokes, puzzles and card games. Very popular in the valley was the barroom sport of arm wrestling, for most of the patrons were men of muscle, lumberjacks, sawmill hands, rivermen and farm hands. Might was right.

Every tavern had its own champion. One such champ was Cliff Harvis who claimed he had bested the best men of three taverns upriver. In fact he was called "Cliff the Arm Buster." He bragged he could beat any man on two legs and would bet ten dollars gold on that statement. It was over at Batchellerville where with brawn, leverage and special flick of the wrist he proved how dangerous he could be.

Cliff and the local champ of Helltown Tavern were locked in a viselike grip when Cliff put on enormous pressure on the humerus bone of his opponent and there came a sound like a gunshot. The loud crack was a snapped bone, busted like a stout branch of a tree.

The arm flapped uselessly to the man's side, broke clean above the elbow. The bet was won and there was the shattered arm to prove it. Cliff picked up the bet. There was silence in the bar as a coat was placed around the shoulders of the loser and he was led away by two friends to seek help at the local doctor.

Cliff said, "Too bad he broke his arm, ain't it? Who's

next?" The bar keep went to the other end of the bar. The patrons remained silent but had surly looks. Time passed. Milt Ronshell had his arm in a sling for a long time, but recovered. Of course he hated the man that broke his arm.

Everyone knew that Cliff worked at a sawmill near Dogtown. On the way along the river from the sawmill to the tavern there was a short cut, a narrow path and dangerous "Dead Man's Sands" which had to be crossed by jumping from rock to rock across the quick sands. They were reported to be bottomless, as were some of the bogs in treacherous Big Vly. A sign had been erected at both sides of the dangerous crossing of the sands.

I was told that one day in early winter when the days are short and darkness comes in early, Milt Ronshell was seen driving a lone ox and an ox cart toward the sawmill from Dogtown. Someone remarked that was a strange way for him to go. Even though he lived on the other side of the river, surely he knew of the sands and that the ox couldn't hop from rock to rock. Later, after dark, the jangle of the chains of the ox and cart were heard and they knew Milt had turned around when he came upon the sands.

Cliff always came to the tavern to drink, play cards and brag about his arm wrestling. He didn't show up at the tavern that night. Nor did he show up for work at the mill next morn. In fact he didn't show up for work the next couple of days. Pay night came and some of the fellers with their pockets jingling with gold and silver coins took a lantern from the mill and decided to take the shortcut to Dogtown and the tavern.

They reached Dead Man's Sands and the first man started across, but stopped on a rock. "Hey fellers," he yelled. "Stop! One of the rocks has been moved."

"What do you mean?" someone questioned.

"Why I can tell it's been moved by the look of it and

159

the position it's in. Someone get close with that lantern, in case that rock ain't set right. I'm gonna hop to it."

He did and went on. They all crossed safely. The last feller to get to solid ground had a coal oil lantern and saw a hat at the edge of the dangerous sands. He picked it up.

"This here is the hat Cliff Harris always wore."

The men looked at it, then took it with them to the tavern. After a few drinks, some of them went back to the sands.

By the light of a couple of lanterns they saw tracks of just the ox, that stopped at the edge of the quagmire, and then turned around. They saw the marks of a chain, and one man went out on the rocks used as safe stepping stones. He was sure he saw the mark of a chain on one rock, and was sure the rock had been moved. They went back to the Tavern and got the Town constable. They showed him the hat and told him Cliff hadn't been seen in days.

The constable went with the men to the sands and looked at tracks and such. The next day he rode his horse across the river to question Milt Ronshell. But he did not learn anything, and he did not have any real proof that Milt had caused the disappearance of Clint.

It was figured that Cliff, always so sure of himself, had in the gloom of early night gone bounding across the rocks, and had jumped as usual for the fourth rock. But it was not in place and he plunged into the quicksands that swallowed him up, leaving just his hat floating on top. They were sure Milt had moved the rock, but no one had enough proof.

The hat of Cliff Harris was hung on a peg in the wall of the tavern. I was told it hung there for years and years, a memory of "Cliff the Arm Buster."

SOME GHOSTS
OF THE VALLEY

I wonder if more ghost stories were told in the valley than there were ghosts.

The quiet house, bumps in the night, footsteps on the stairway when no one was there, chains rattling in the basement. Footfalls heard behind you on the quiet road as look around to see no one there. The will-o'-the-wisps dancing in the night near the creek. I guess it was easy to believe in ghosts back then, 'cause even some older folks were not convinced that spirits were not constantly around intruding in the happenings of every day life.

There were tales about grisly events up and down the valley. Most happened years ago and had grown into veritable legends with all the telling and retelling. Let me share a few with you.

There's the sad story of the feller that had an argument with his girl near Paul's Creek, just at dusk, as he was walking her home from the store at Huntsville. The mill was running, grinding some buckwheat for a farmer who'd arrived late. As I was told, they had an argument—the feller and girl. He swung away from the girl and either slipped or jumped into the raceway and was carried down by the water turning the big wheel. That there mill wheel kinda chopped him up right smart, before the miller could use the shut-off. What was left of the young feller was buried.

But anytime after that if the mill was running late in the day, especially of a fall or winter day when the sun set early in the eventide and night closed in on the land, the spirit of that feller would appear in the raceway as the water turned the mill wheel. That went on for years, till the grist mill burned down.

Then there was Old Jeremiah. He was called Jerry, the Ghost of Meeting House Corner. Seems that Jerry when he was alive, feared of being buried alive if he had a stroke. That was before the days of embalming a body. So Old Jerry got his best friend to promise to do something for him when the final hour came, when they could feel no pulse and his breath didn't cloud up a hand mirror held to his nose and mouth and they said, "Poor Jerry is dead!" The friend was to slash Poor Jerry's wrists with a sharp razor and let the blood drain out. That way he'd make sure that Jerry was finished in this life.

Well, Jerry's time came. The friend took the razor, stood next the bed, said, "God help me, Jerry old friend. I can't do it."

Jerry was buried in the graveyard at Meeting House Corner. But his spirit returned to the buryin' ground and was seen there shakin' its hands as if lookin' for the completion of the promise that had been made. Jerry's friend who had made the promise was told about Jerry's ghost. That friend, name of Tracy Odom, was a woman. She went to the graveyard. Sure enough, she saw Old Jerry's haunt. She shrieked and ran into the night.

The next morn the preacher saw her body swingin' from a wide- branched oak tree in the church yard. The preacher had the body cut down, but did not want the body of a suicide buried in his graveyard. Nevertheless, a deacon had her buried there and the ghost of Poor Old Jerry seen no more.

Dutch Jake of Frog Town was a river driver who worked at getting the logs down river to the mill. Jake got drowned in the river. They fished his body out.

162

Jake was a man who always wore two pairs of long johns. But when the barber-carpenter-undertaker laid out Jake, his wife only gave him one pair of drawers to dress the body, keeping the other pair to give to a nephew.

"Jake," she said, "sure won't be a-needin' them."

Jake was buried. But most every night the ghost of Dutch Jake came to the house and the widow, she got upset. She moved to another shack on the river, but the ghost followed her. She moved again and the ghost followed her once more. Now she was real scared. So the widow talked to a granny woman. The witch told her that Jake's soul was restless and was lookin' for something.

"Next time he appears, you speak right out. Don't scream or cry. Just ask Jake what it is that he seeks in the name of the Lord?"

That very night the ghost of Jake appeared to the widow. She was scared but remembered what the witch told her. She spoke out, "Jake, please, what in the name of the Lord do you want?"

A voice then said, "Nancy, give me another pair of drawers!"

So Nancy, the widow, told the witch. The witch went with her to the graveyard. There the two women scooped out a little hole on the mound of Jake's grave, put in a pair of Long Johns and covered them up with grave dirt.

From then on Dutch Jake rested in his grave!

PART FIVE:

A U N T   W I L M A

AUNT WILMA, WITCH LADY

"You might laugh. But my Aunt was a sure enough witch lady." That's what old Clayton Yates of Stewart's Bridge told me. I didn't laugh. Not only because I was working for him. You don't laugh at the Boss Man if you got any sense, for he pays you. It was also because if you lauhg at what someone says you'll probably hear no more of the story. I was young and wanted to learn all I could. I still do, for that matter.

Mister Clayton told such interesting stories that I felt I was right back in those old days. His stories were better than reading a book it seemed, and there were very few books in the valley seventy years ago. There were coal oil lanterns to see and read by if one wanted. But most people worked, ate, and slept.

Clayton told me that his Aunt Wilma had a house between Conklinville and the Croweville area. She was a widow lady. Her man had been workin' logs comin' down river when a sudden bad storm broke up the raft. He was broke up, too.

Those days they not only had the big log drives downriver on the spring snow melt. Other times they brought hardwood logs to the mills and factories. There was beech, maple, ash, and even chestnut, which grew aplenty back then before the blight killed 'em off. They made large rafts, with about every third or fourth log a pine or spruce which were soft woods and floated better and helped move the other logs. The float logs were used most any time of spring, summer and fall if the water wasn't low in summer or froze over in winter.

167

So that's why there were stories of men killed on the river.

Of course they also got killed in the lumber work in the forests. Killed by a tree, falling down a cliff, horse-kicked or by a log rolling on them. (A log broke my left foot once). Anyway, all work was by hand, axe, cross-cut saw, wedges, log chains and such. There were no safety laws then. You kept alert and took your chances.

Anyway, Aunt Wilma was a granny Woman and witch lady. Aunt Wilma said one of the worst things she did in witchery was to send a bunch of dead flowers to the Church to be given to a young bride-to-be as she stood before the preacher. She attached a hand printed note that read "Posies for your wedding day— An omen for your future."

The young girl took those awful flowers, read the note, screamed and dropped dead.

There was a big scandal and hate for the jealous girl who'd hired Wilma to do that. People hated Wilma for that, too, but at the same time, more folks came sneaking around to her house to have fortunes told, buy charms and amulets and herbs and pay for predictions and such like.

Clayton said when he was a little boy she got him to catch frogs, shoot bats and bring her snakes. These were mostly dried by his Aunt, who also cut off chicken feet, which she had hanging from strings. He claimed she had a live rabbit that did things for her like a little person. Clayton said his Aunt could change into the "Bird of Wisdom", an Owl and fly on nights of the full moon. But he admitted to me he never saw that happen.

Aunt Wilma could make people well when they were sick. He remembered once a man was splittin' firewood kindling, missed or misjudged, and whacked off the top joint of his thumb as he held a chunk. People brought the man to Wilma with the man's bleeding hand

168

wrapped in rags. Wilma washed the hand with something out of a bottle, ran outdoors and got some puff ball mushrooms, then squirted the dry spores onto the cut-off stub of the thumb. Then she stuck the stub in a hole she made in another puff ball, tied the puff ball to the hand with clean cloths and told everyone, "There will be no more blood." The man's hand healed and he was known thereafter as "Nine Finger Jack." Many's the time I've thought of that story when I've kicked a puff ball in the woods to see it squirt.

Aunt Wilma had a big black shaggy dog that roamed the countryside and woods. Sometimes it was gone for days. I remember it because it was a strange name for a dog, or for anything. The dog was called "Moggy Dhoo." Clayton said he never knew what the name meant. Some sort of witch name. Aunt Wilma told him the dog could run on water and once he thought he saw it do just that.

One time, Wilma had some folk in the barn. They had just cut the throat of a black goat and were drinking the blood when a man came up behind Clayton and kicked him away from a crack in the barn where he was peeking. Clayton ran home crying and his mother told him to stay away from Aunt Wilma's—but he'd sneak back whenever he could.

Clayton once saw his Aunt and another woman carry a man out of the house to the barn. He thought it was a dead man. Next morning, though, he saw the man. He'd just been drunk.

COHORT OF SATAN

Clayton told me that his Aunt Wilma used to make a love potion that she sold. A feller was supposed to get his girl to drink it. From then on, she only thought of him. Same with a girl, if she could get the feller to drink it. Clayton said he drank some himself and chased after a couple girls. Finally took one as his wife.

"I didn't know," he said. "till some time later that along with the herbs, honey and rain water in the drink, Aunt Wilma had put in the potion some stuff from a bull that don't come from no cows!"

One time Aunt Wilma had a woman cross her palm with silver because the woman wanted Wilma to "smite her no good man with a curse so he'd not chase young girls no more."

That night there was a Thunder Boomer and a large maple next the couple's house was smitten by lightning and wind and toppled over. The fallen tree did damage to the house, of course. It also did damage to the husband. Crippled him up so that he could hardly walk no more, nor chase the girls.

Wilma got credit for that. She was then spoken of as a Cohort of Satan. Friend of the Lord of the Gates of Death. Clayton said folks spoke ill of Aunt Wilma but continued to see her at her house near Mad Run, a small stream that ran down to the river.

Then the preacher Man began to sell a sort of a little medal to wear around the neck, ca Talisman against witchcraft. Those folks that refused to buy it, providing money for the Church, were denounced as favoring witchcraft.

Aunt Wilma laughed and told little Clayton the preacher Man was a "witch Finder" like in the old days. Clayton said he had one of those Talisman medals; he also had a little red wool pouch, and an amulet on a leather thong he always wore around his neck, an amulet given him by aunt Wilma. He said he felt funny wearing them both as they favored two different ways of thinking. He wondered if he fell in the river and drowned if he'd go to Heaven or to Hell?

Aunt Wilma also sold Hooch, Moonshine or Stump Juice that she bought from a feller up on the mountain. She also had a young girl that worked at keeping house for her and was learning to become a witch. The girl also served drinks and shared favors with some of the mem that came to the house, from the woods, river and farms and sawmills.

One night, of a full moon, the Aunt went into a back bedroom and closed the old door, leaving the girl and a feller in the front room. The man had been drinking, he quietly followed the Aunt and peeked through a crack in the door. He told next day that he'd seen the witch take off her clothes and rub herself all over with some grease from a can. Then she turned into an owl and flew out the open window.

This excited the lumberjack. He got the girl to go into the room and steal the can of grease for him. She did. He put the grease on himself but he didn't turn into an owl. He turned into a wolf and rushed out the door. The girl had taken the wrong can of grease.

The wolfman ran up the valley in the moonlight. A farmer who was out hunting coons, saw what he thought was a wolf and shot at it, wounding it in the leg. The next morning, after the moon had set behind the mountain and the sun was rising, the lumberjack was found near the river. He had been shot in the leg and told a crazy story about being a wolf. Some folks said he must have been drunk.

Clayton said after that people were more fearful of Aunt Wilma but still went to see her. I says to him, "If you tell that to a Jackass he'll kick your brains out." We both laughed at that old expression.

Still laughing he told me that his Aunt Wilma could even turn a man into a mule or horse and ride him up and down the valley roads on a night of a full moon!

Wilma used cards called Tarot Cards which can be used to play card games. But Wilma used them for fortune telling called divination. Clayon remembered a man had been to the doctor at Fish House who said he had a kidney condition, gave him pills and couldn't cure him. The feller went to Wilma who gave him herbs and then sat on his back. He got cured.

She treated the deaf, the crippled, those with chest and heart pains, sickness, broken bones and injuries, frost bite, She stopped bleeding and cured all kinds of ailments.

Aunt Wilma, Clayton said, was a great woman.

JINX REMOVING POWDER

The belief was that a witch was very fearful of getting into any kind of a personal fight, because if she lost any blood—even a few drops from a scratch—she lost her mystical powers till the next full moon.

True spells, it was believed, do exist as well as many fake ones. The actual force or magic of the witch was not in words or things she used, it was within the witch. Even now as I write and you read, possibly real spells are being used every day? Old spells, perhaps. have no more power than new ones. Who knows?

Clayton told how one time a woman who accused Aunt Wilma of putting a hex on her, caused illness in herself, the cow to go dry and the chickens to stop laying eggs.

The woman attacked Aunt Wilma, charged at her with a knife that she had hidden in her bosom. The woman was real upset and shouting that she would cut Wilma and drain all her Devil's blood from her. Aunt Wilma quick-like grabbed a pillow and shoved it into her attacker's face. The woman struggled for breath and fell to the floor. Then Wilma sat on her and tied her hands with the colored witch cord she wore around her waist as a witch belt. Later, after she talked with the woman and gave her a drink of herb tea and Jinx Removing Powder, the lady calmed down.

Aunt Wilma explained that some other witch lady had placed a hex or cast the Evil Eye on her. Then Aunt Wilma gave the lady a red flannel amulet to wear around her neck on a rawhide thong. The amulet or pouch was filled with herbs and charm pebbles from a

special pool in the river. That would ward off evil. The lady went home satisfied—and after that Aunt Wilma always made sure to have a pillow handy when anyone came to her house.

When I was working for Clayton in 19 and 27 as a drover with his oxen at Stewarts Bridge (after the war the bridge was taken down and that was the site for the second dam on the Sacandaga) I remember an old man brought a dun mare to Clayton and asked him to destroy the worms in the horse as Aunt Wilma would have done. Clayton mostly had oxen but knew horses and mules also. I was interested for I knew horses. My Pop had a carriage horse when I was a little tad and I took care of it.

Clayton got some dry herbs he had hanging up in a shed. Used some catnip, coltsfoot and such. Mixed it with some ground oats and fed it to the mare. Then, being but part pow wow Doctor, he said a prayer, something like this, to the horse.

"If you have any worms, I will take your forelock. If they be white, brown, or red, they shall and must be dead."

After that he shook the mare's head three times, passed his hand over the back three times, to and fro and did the same thing three times on the belly. Then he gave the man the mare. The next week the man came back and gave Clayton a goat's milk cheese. The worms were gone. Clayton gave me a chunk of the cheese to take to my camp. It was tasty.

I'll add here that Dry Coltsfoot herb rolled in paper and smoked for a few days, usually will cure a person of smoking!

"CAREFUL! YOU MAY NOT MAKE IT PAST THE NIGHT!"

After Clayton had gotten into telling me about his early days, he'd tell me more about his Aunt Wilma the witch—as long as I did not laugh at his stories.

He told of the time when some feller—a warlock—from Denton's Corners rode on his cloud horse and brought much needed wind and rain to the valley so that the heavy rains would refresh the earth, streams and river. They also talked of the big, white doe that leaped in great jumps through the forests of the mountains. Anyone seeing it, and *not* shooting at it, would have a wish come true. Over on one of the mountains across the river, there was a large white buck deer. When seen it foretold of danger being near—illness, accident, sometimes even death.

Clayton, even as an old man, believed that there was still a pack of witch hounds that ran the woods in Tile Austin's Mountain. Anyone that heard them could make a wish and it would come true. He claimed he'd had several wishes come true after he heard the witch hounds in the night. He wondered when he died how his future would be? He believed from his Aunt that souls do not perish at death of a person. They go from the body of death—to a new life in a baby being born, or an animal, even a bird. Reincarnation. He said sometimes his dreams took him back into other lives that he had probably lived. And he hadn't read of being in those places. Said once he dreamed of all kinds of strange animals.

177

He told me that some folks that were friends of his and believed in the witches of the valley had had their own marriage which near as I can remember was called something like "Tailltenn Marriage." They said, "Do not bother Priest or preacher with your private union and affairs. Live your own life." But Clayton married his own wife in front of a preacher. The girl wouldn't have it any other way. He was glad that he did. They had many great years together.

On May 1st called Beltane Day, a witch day in the spring, they built two outdoor bonfires apart from each other and drove all the cattle, sheep, goats and pigs, and led the horses and mules between the two fires for breeding and prevention against sickness. Herbs and roots were put on the hot coals. This was free and many valley folks brought their stock to those fires. Sometimes a Maw and Paw and six or eight kids brought their stock to the May Day Bonfires. There was no charge for this. People also brought food and drink and there was eating and sharing, music, dancing talk and visiting, games and contests, races and such. There was even swimming if the river water wasn't too cold. There would be several witch ladies and they made predictions and told fortunes in tea cups, read hand lines and special tellings from their private stone. Lots of fun.

But one May Day brought a sad happening. A preacher came to the gathering and called the witch ladies and every one there, bad names and said they were all evil and Devil Worship trash. And he spit on one of the fires where food was cooking. Tess Berry the witch lady from Deadwood Clearing stood up and near as I can remember, said, "preacher Man, you've had your say. Careful. You many not make it past the night."

He didn't. Clayton said that preacher died in bed before the sun rose in the morn.

THE GODS ARE NOT
ALL POWERFUL

As I've mentioned before, Clayton told me that his Aunt Wilma was a witch lady. That was something his Dad, brother to Wilma, did not seem to take any interest in, one way or t'other. But his Ma, being from a different kind of family, was against Clayton's being trained to be a Warlock, a male witch. So his Ma always made sure he went to church every Sunday morning and also to Bible Talk, most Wednesday nights.

But there was, for the young boy, mystery, excitement, and things to see, hear and do at Aunt Wilma's house. So Clayton sneaked off there whenever he could. Even though he'd probably get, "a scoldin' and a whuppin' if his Maw found out." he said. "But it was wuth it!" he added.

Not all witch women were hags. I myself knew one, a kindly, aged lady who lived with her Owl and her dog. I have a snapshot, faded now, that I took about 68 years ago. She was another person displaced by the building of the first dam and the flooding of the valley. Some witch-women, I was told, were very pretty girls when young.

Clayton told me that something happened when he was a little lad that he would have like to have seen. There was a very, very dry summer. Hot and dry winds. There was hardly any water flowing in the river, many shallows. Pools and large boulders showed that usually were under water. Hayfields were dry, bleached white. Corn, potatoes, gardens and such were in terrible

179

shape. Small streams dried up and there were fires in the dry forests on the mountains.

Some folks got together and implored a granny lady to use some sort of uncanny powers or some such to bring rain to the valley. The witch lady got in touch with a couple of others to work with her. On the night of the first full moon, they built a large bonfire on a flat near the river. They put on branches of green leaves to make smoke and added different kinds of herbs. There was a group of folks there and the head witch, the other witches and some young girls and women took off their clothes and danced around the fire, saying chants. The fire gave off clouds of smoke to the skies above. More and more leaves and weeds and brush went onto the fire.

Then the dancers threw handfuls of water on one another from some pails of spring water, put on their clothes and killed a black goat. Each drank a sip of blood from a clay cup from the slashed throat of the animal. Carrying burning pine branches they formed a circle around the fire and did more chanting. When the fire burned down, they broke up the gathering just as the lead witch said, "The moon shall set. There will be no sunrise, for there shall be rain and all will rejoice!"

It is very seldom that it rains on the night of a full moon but the very next morning there came heavy showers upon the valley. From then on, there were regular summer showers. The river waters rose, crops regained some of their growth. The rains were life-giving and the people had more respect for the witches.

What really happened? Only the flowing river and brooding forests knew the answer to the question. Did unseen powers exist and bring forth the precious rains from Heaven? Clayton told me that, whatever did it, the rains came in time to save the valley.

As I remember it, he said that his Aunt Wilma told him, "The gods are not all-powerful. They need the help of some women to remind them that mortals here on earth must not be forgotten!"

I didn't know whether to believe all he'd told me on snowy days when we made repairs to ox yokes, chains and various gear in the barn. But it sure gave me a many a thing to remember!

CASTING A CURSE

Clayton told me that sometimes, to please a person that gave her a gift as a request for evil against some particular person, his Aunt Wilma would make a sort of doll out of an old stocking and some rags with buttons sewed on for eyes. Or maybe she'd fashion a rough little human figure of wax or clay from the Clay Pit. Others knew of the Clay Pits besides the Indians. She then made a skirt to put on a woman figure, or a hat for a man figure.

The idea was first to let the word get out by gossip that the particular person had an enemy who sought evil against her or him and that the Powers of Darkness were being called upon. That scared the person the curse was put on. Then the witch would take some herbs and work herself into a rage. Depending on the request made of her, the witch would steep the doll in some sort of herb tea, or slowly burn it next to a fire.

If the figure was wax she would stick pins in it for pain, or slowly melt part or all of it, next to a lighted candle, depending on the curse. The clay figure, if used, would be given a broken arm or leg or the back would be scraped with the edge of a dull knife to give back pains to the intended victim.

Clayton said many times the curse would work. His Aunt Wilma would tell him or he would hear about it up at the store. But, Clayton said, if the intended victim could have a White witch, or a pow wow Doctor act in time, the intended curse could be shunned and avoided. He had faith in the doings of witches and pow wow Doctors of his early days.

A person could be stopped from talking gossip, or bad, about another person if a witch would pin the lips together of one of her dolls by using a couple of thorns from a blackberry bush. Or one might be stopped form using force against another person if a wax or clay figure was tightly bound with string. Clayton told me a wife could visit a witch and have the witch stop the hubby from beating a wife or kids.

The figures made by witches were called "Poppets," used to place or cast a curse or spell on a person. Sometimes in special cases a large Poppet was made of rags, placed on top the chimney and burned.

Clayton had so much information about his Aunt Wilma and other witch Women and pow wow Doctors. I could never hear enough of it. Clayton told me that a witch-made figure or image could also be used to cure sickness and injury of human or animals. Even with the patient at a distance, once the figure was complete, the witch made prayers or incantations and put herb remedies in or on the figure and cast her thoughts so that they made a link across the miles. And oft times the patient recovered. Of course, if they died, that meant evil had stepped in and the fate was determined. The patient would then be buried in a churchyard with prayers. Fate!

Perhaps a farmer wanted his wheat to grow and be fruitful. Aunt Wilma then made a doll of wheat straw from his barn and propped it against the entrance to the stone wall that encircled his wheat field, sprinkled the straw doll with powdered Deer Horn and Lucky Hand Root. After that, the field produced a very good crop of wheat, more than his neighbors' fields did.

A few times a wagon train of Gypsies came to the valley, looking to trade horses, mules, sheep and goats. They seemed to be a happy people. Clayton said what struck him most was the Gypsy custom to leap over a broom at weddings. I can recall Gypsy camps and the colorful painted wagons, horse drawn, the herds of horses and mules, the fancy colored clothes of the people. Then the wagons were replaced with automobiles and trucks. Even later in the 19 and 20's I can remember the campfires at what was called the Gypsy campgrounds on the Hudson River riverbank, on the Luzerne side, just below Hadley-Luzerne. It is now called the River Road. That camp ground was also used by the river drivers when the spring log drives came down river. (I also remember, not long after WWII, the last spring drive of 10,000 cords of peeled pulp wood down the Hudson.)

There was an old, local custom in the valley of a form of marriage over a broomstick. That was usually done in the winter when the travelling Parson could not get through the snows and intense freezing weather. Most of the valley was locked in, come wintertime.

That kind of a broomstick union was not considered binding if either party wanted to default at winter's end. If they were loving and agreeable then they'd get the Parson to "hitch 'em up" when he came their way in the spring. Sort of an early day trial marriage. But if a child was conceived then it was expected they would wed—unless the feller took off for Canada. Then the girl was spoken of as a "Canada Bride" or a "Broomstick Bride"

Mothers of young girls were usually careful to prevent a daughter from stepping over a broom at home. The belief was that if a girl should step over a broom, she might become a mother before she was a wife. If, by accident, some girl stepped over a broom, a witch was sometimes spoken to. She would give the girl a charm bag to wear around her neck. This bag contained herbs, maybe some powdered bones of a black cat, maybe some bats fur or blood I was told. The witch also gave the girl some herb teas to drink.

If the girl did become with child, she was given a different tea to drink. That was "All Saints Powder," if the baby was wanted or "Devil's Shoestring Powder" if the baby was not wanted. That usually took care of the situation. Perhaps the girl had actually purposely stepped over the broom as her way of announcing a knowledge of birds and bees.

If a baby was born out of wedlock, it was called a "Woods Colt." Sometime I will tell a story about a Woods Colt, in the valley mountains, when the second Sacandaga Dam was being built.

If a man drowned in the river and his body did not soon come to the surface a witch was notified. She would come to the site of the accident bringing a full loaf of bread (before sliced bread). The witch would say a prayer and toss the loaf of bread into the water. It was believed if the body was anywhere nearby that the bread would hover around as it floated. Then several men who had gathered would fire their guns in the air. That was supposed to have an effect on the natural gas forming in the body and cause it to rise. In the large towns, I was told, a cannon was fired across the waters, "to raise the dead!"

The witch also cast an herb called, "John the Conquering Root" into the river. That was supposed to appease the River God the Indians called "Sacandag." It was said that one man whose body was recovered and came back to life, claimed that, "There was a beautiful land at the depths of the river."

Then there was the man who got hurt on the mountain, fell off a cliff and laid unconscious for a couple-three days. When he woke up he was scared. He had his witch charm bag, a leather pouch on a rawhide string around his neck. He rubbed the pouch and prayed. Then a beautiful woman came out of the woods. Her head was crowned with a crescent moon and there was like a flame of pale fire between her hands when she spread them apart. She led him down the mountain to a shack where a woodchopper lived. The man took him in and cared for him for several days. Then he helped him down the mountain to West Day.

Being young, I liked the stories, but I was flippant and said to Clayton, "Gee, that lady must have been fired with kindness."

He'd hardly talk to me for a couple of days. I'd forgot he'd been learning to be a male witch when he was a boy and put great stock and belief in the stories. After that, I again tried not to rile him.

I believe my story has gone on long enough, but since I have you attention here is one more gem I remember and that will bring me to a close. For the uncomfortable and annoying disturbance of hiccups, sit down, with a glass of water at your side.

Say these words: "Oh hiccough, please stop, stop, stop!"

At the same time have someone there with you put a little water in each of your ears with the little, pinky finger of each of their hands, keeping the fingers there in the ears, while you drink all water in the glass,

If that don't work here's the sure cure. Bend your head forward as you stand up. Then bend your body forward so that your hands touch the ground and say, "Oh, hiccough, I wish that you were in my buttocks!"

That'll work if you don't die laughing.

"THE DEVIL'S GOT ME!"

This story was told to me over fifty years ago by Clayton Yates of Stewart's Bridge.

Clayton had a cousin who lived down the river in Hadley Town. That cousin had a nice horse he wanted to sell, so he put the word out that the horse was for sale. This horse was kept in a large wooden stall with high sides at the front part of the barn. The stall was large enough for the horse to lay down. A Frenchman came to look at the horse and spent some time with it. He liked the horse, asked the price, then said that he'd have to think it over and went away.

Later that same day, a man came along with a large, fully- grown, very tame black bear on a leash. The pair went from town to town putting on a show. They'd work in exchange for a place to sleep. That was the custom with travellers in those days. So the cousin moved the horse to a stall at the back part of the barn and they tied the bear in the front stall with a long rope from his neck collar so he could move around, stand up and lay down. The man was to sleep in an extra room in the house and was also given supper and breakfast.

There was some moon that night, enough to give a bit of light in the barn, but not enough to really see what was to be seen. About 2:00 A.M. there was an awful commotion in the barn. Someone was yelling, horses were whinnying and kicking the stalls, the chickens were squawking and the bear was growling.

The cousin and the bear's owner were aroused, quick put on some clothes, took lanterns and rushed out to the barn where the trouble was. They found the bear

standing up on his hind legs, with his front paws around the Frenchman, who was yelling at the top of his lungs. When the Frenchman saw the two men with lanterns in the doorway of the barn, he screamed, "The Devil's got me! The Devil!"

The bear trainer gave a command and the bear let go of his prisoner and dropped to his four feet. The two men quieted the horses and took the Frenchman outside the barn. In the lamplight they saw he was unharmed but scared. Nearly scared to death, he was shaking so much that he was almost crying. The scared man admitted that he had planned to come back and steal the horse he had looked at when he was there before. Not knowing that the horse had been moved, he went into the stall with the bear. In the gloom he didn't realize he'd made a mistake and the bear grabbed him in a bear hug.

He said he was sure that the Devil had him. All he could see was what he thought was a big man with long arms covered with thick, long hair, steam coming from his nose and eyes that glared fire. He pleaded for mercy and swore that he would never, never, steal again. The two men decided to let him go, as the fright had been punishment enough. But they told him to leave town and never come back.

They returned to the house to make some coffee, laugh and talk. And that was the Hadley Bear Story!

THE OLD HORNED GOD

Some folks thought that the Great Horned Owl that flew the night skies on silent wings, was a devil's imp, come to the valley foretelling trouble!"

If such an owl was shot and put on display at the store or even the Church, people would stare at the the big black and yellow eyes and finger the horns which were only feathers and wonder if it were truly only a night bird and not a Demon with horns.

The witches claimed it was the "Old Horned God" of England and also Scotland, where many of their ancestors came from. Remember that in the early day of the settlement of the valley there were still English coins that had been hidden away. Sometimes they were still offered at stores in making a purchase or in paying a debt. Old customs died slowly. In fact I had several of those English coins that I saved from the valley.

Some winters the weather to the north must have been severe. For then we would have the Snowy Owls of the north visit us. I can remember them sitting on top of fence posts. Some people believed the Snow Owls were also bad spirits, foretellers of a killing winter. And of course it was the bad northern winters that sent them to the valley and around Porter Corners and South Corinth where I lived. Now the stories of the Old Horned God are gone. But the horned owls remain.

BIBLIOGRAPHY

ANALYSIS, CLASSIFICATION AND THEORY

Aarne, Antti. *The Types of the Folk-Tale: A Classification and Bibliography.* Translated by Stith Thompson. New York: Burt Franklin, 1971.

Arrowsmith, Nancy. *A Field Guide to the Little People.* New York: Pocket Books, 1977.

Bateson, Gregory. *Mind and Nature: A Necessary Unity.* New York: Bantam Books, 1979.

Baroja, J. Caro. *The World of Witches.* Chicago, 1964.

Baughman, Ernest W. *Type and Motif Index of the Folktales of England and North America.* Bloomington: Folklore Institute of Indiana University, 1966.

Bernheimer, R. *Wild Men in the Middle Ages : A. Study in Art, Sentiment and Demonology.* Cambridge, Mass.: Harvard University Press, 1952.

Boatwright, Mody. *The Family Saga and Other Phases of American Folklore.* Urbana, Illinois, 1958.

Brownlaw, Louis. *The Anatomy of the Anecdote.* Chicago, 1960.

Cohen, Daniel. *The Encyclopedia of the Strange.* New York: Avon Books, 1985.

Cohn, Norman. *Europe's Inner Demons: An Enquiry Inspired by the Great Witch-Hunt.* New York: Basic Books, 1975.

Cooper, J.C. *Dictionary of Symbolic and Mythological Animals.* San Francisco: Harper Collins, 1992.

194

Dorson, Richard M. *Peasant Customs and Savage Myths.* London: Oxford University Press, 1968.

Dundes, Alan. *Interpreting Folklore.* Bloomington: Indiana University Press, 1980.

Estes, Clarissa Pinkola. *Women Who Run with the Wolves: Myths and Stories of the Wild Woman Archetype.* New York: Ballentine Books, 1992.

Faust, Albert B. *The German Element in the United States.* New York: The Steuben Society of America, 1927.

Frazer, Sir James George. *The Golden Bough: A Study of Magic and Religion.* New York: The MacMillan Company, 1958.

Gioseffi, Daniela, ed. *On Prejudice: A Global Perspective.* New York and London: Doubleday Anchor, 1993.

Graves, Robert. *The White Goddess: A Historical Grammar of Poetic Myth.* Peter Smith Publishers. Amended and enlarged edition, 1983. Reprint. Noonday Press, 1997.

Holbrook, Stewart. *The Yankee Exodus.* New York: MacMillan, 1950.

Kightly, Charles. *The Customs and Ceremonies of Britain: An Encyclopedia of Living Traditions.* London: Thames and Hudson, 1986.

Kittredge, Lyman. *Witchcraft in Old and New England.* Cambridge, Mass.: Harvard University Press, 1929.

Kramer, Frank R. *Voices in the Valley: Mythmaking and Folk Belief in the Shaping of the Middle West.* Madison: University of Wisconsin Press, 1964.

Langer, Suzanne. *Philosophy in a New Key.* Cambridge, Mass.: Harvard University Press, 1942.

Loomis, C. Grant. *White Magic: An Introduction to the Folklore of Christian Legend.* Cambridge, Mass.: The Medieval Academy of America, 1948.

Miller, Perry. *The New England Mind.* New York: MacMillan, 1939.

O'Suilleabhain, Sean. *A Handbook of Irish Folklore.* Dublin: The Folklore Society of Ireland, 1942.

Snyder, Richard C. and H. Hubert Wilson. *The Roots of Political Behavior.* New York: American Book Company, 1949.

195

Tart, G. *Altered States of Consciousness*. New York, 1962.

Taylor, Archer. "The Biographical Pattern in Traditional Narrative." *Journal of the Folklore Institute*. Volume I (1964).

Thompson, Stith. *The Folktale*. New York: Holt, Rinehart and Winston, 1946.

Vansina, Jan. *Oral Tradition as History*. Madison: University of Wisconsin Press, 1985.

Walker, Barbara G. *The Woman's Encyclopedia of Myths and Secrets*. San Francisco: Harper-San Francisco, 1983.

Warner, Marina. *From the Beast to the Blonde: On Fairy Tales and Their Tellers*. New York: Farrar, Strauss, and Giroux, 1994.

_____. *No Go the Bogeyman: Scaring, Lulling, and Making Mock*. New York: Farrar, Strauss, and Giroux, 1998.

Wells, Evelyn K. *The Ballad Tree*. New York: The Ronald Press, 1950.

FICTION AND NARRATIVE POETRY

Bradley, Marion Zimmer, Robert E. Howard, Manley Wade Wellman, et al. *Ghor, Kin-Slayer: The Saga of Gensaric's Fifth-Born Son.*, 1997.

Curran, Rondla, ed. *The Weird Gathering and Other Tales from the Enchanted World of Dark Legends: "Supernatural" Women in American Popular Fiction, 1800–1850*. New York: Fawcett Crest, 1979.

DeFoe, Daniel. *The True Relation of the Apparition of One Mr. Veal*, 1706.

Fortune, Dion. *Demon Lover*. Samuel Weiser reprint, 1980.

_____. *The Sea Priestess*. Samuel Weiser reprint, 1979.

Gottscalck, Frederick. "The Witch Dance on the Bracken." *Burton's Gentleman's Magazine*. Volume VII (November, 1840).

Kaye, Marvin. *The Penguin Book of Witches and Warlocks: Tales of Black Magic Old and New*. New York: Penguin Books, 1991.

Radford, Ken. *Fire Burn: Tales of Witchcraft*. New York: Peter Bedrick Books, 1989.

Wellman, Manley Wade, *The Hanging Stones*. out of print.

Whittier, John Greenleaf. *Legends of New England*. Hartford, 1831.

FOLKLORE

Booker, L.R. *Ghosts and Witches of Martin County*. Williamson, NC., 1971.

Botkin, B.A. ed. *A Treasury of American Folklore*. New York: American Legacy Press, 1964.

Brewer, J. Mason. *Dog Ghosts: The Word on the Brazos*. Austin: University of Texas Press, 1958, 1976.

Briggs, Katherine. "A Dictionary of British Folktales in the English Language." *Journal of the Folklore Institute*. Volume II (1965).

——. *An Encyclopedia of Fairies, Hobgoblins, Brownies, Bogies, and Other Supernatural Creatures*. New York: Pantheon Books, 1976.

——. *British Folk Tales and Legends: A Sampler*. London: Granada Publishing, 1977, 1978, 1980.

Brunvand, Jan Harold. *The Study of American Folklore: An Introduction*. New York and London: W.W. Norton, 1968, 1978.

——. *The Vanishing Hitchhiker: American Urban Legends and Their Meanings*. New York and London: W.W. Norton and Company, 1981.

Creighton, Helen and Edward Ives. "Eight Folktales from Miramichi as Told by Wilmot MacDonald." *New England Folklore*. Volume IV (1963).

Croker, Thomas Crofton. *Fairy Legends and Traditions of the South of Ireland*. London, 1838.

Daly, John Graham. *The Darker Superstitions of Scotland*. Glasgow, 1835.

Delarue, Paul, ed. *The Borzoi Book of French Folk Tales*. New York, Alfred A. Knopf, 1956.

Dockery Young, Richard and Judy. *The Scary Story Reader.* Little Rock: August House, 1993.

Dorson, Richard. "Oral Styles of American Folk Narratives." *Folklore in Action.* Horace P. Beck, ed. Philadelphia, 1962.

Douglas, Sheila. *The King o' the Black Art and Other Folk Tales.* Aberdeen, Scotland: Aberdeen University Press, 1987.

Hale, C. "Superstitions and Beliefs of the Sea." *Folklore.* Volume 78 (1967), pp. 184–189.

Hand, Wayland, ed. *American Folk Legends: A Symposium.* Berkeley: University of California Press, 1979.

Ireland, G.S. "Legends of Our Lakes." *The Irish Digest.* Volume 68 (1960).

Jagendorf, M. *New England Bean-Pot: American Folk Stories to Read and Tell.* Eau Claire, Wisconsin: E.M. Hale and Company, 1948.

Lindahl, Carl et al, eds. *Swapping Stories: Folktales from Louisiana.* Jackson, Mississippi: University Press of Mississippi, 1997.

Musick, Ruth Ann. *The Telltale Lilac Bush and Other West Virginia Ghost Stories.* Lexington, KY, 1965.

Randolph, Vance. *Hot Springs and Hell.* Hatboro, 1965.

_____. *Ozark Magic and Folklore.* New York: Dover, 1964. Reprint of *Ozark Superstitions.* New York: Columbia University Press, 1947.

Robertson, R. MacDonald. *Selected Highland Folktales.* Nairn, Scotland: David St. John Thomas, 1961, 1977, 1993.

St. Leger-Gordon, Ruth E. *Witchcraft and Folklore of Dartmoor.* New York: Bell Publishing Company, 1972.

Ward, Donald, ed. *The German Legends of the Brothers Grimm, Vol. I.* Philadelphia: Institute for the Study of Human Issues, 1981. Forward by Dan Ben-Amos.

Williamson, Duncan. *May the Devil Walk Behind Ye: Scottish Traveler Tales.* Edinburgh, Scotland: Cannongate Publishing, 1989.

_____. *The Brownies, Sulkies and Fairies: Traveler Tales by Duncan Williamson.* Edinburgh: Cannongate Publishing Ltd., 1985.

Wood, Barbara Allen. *The Devil in Dog Form*. Berkeley: University of California Folklore Studies No. 11, 1959.

Yeats, W.B. *The Celtic Twilight*. New York: Signet Classics, 1986 reprint of 1893 edition.

———, ed. *A Treasury of Irish Myth, Legend, and Folklore: Fairy and Folk Tales of the Irish Peasantry*. New York: Gramercy Books, 1986 reprint.

Yolen, Jane, ed. *Favorite Folktales from Around the World*. New York: Pantheon Books, 1986.

FOLK MEDICINE AND FOLK RELIGION

Beck, Horace P. *Gluskap the Liar and Other Indian Tales*. Freeport Maine: Cumberland Press, Inc., 1966.

Carter, Isabella G. "Mountain White Folk-Lore." *Journal of American Folklore*. Volume 38 (1925).

Dorson, Richard. *Bloodstoppers and Bearwalkers: Folk Tales of Immigrants, Lumberjacks, and Indians*. Cambridge, Mass., and London,: Harvard University Press, 1952.

Ehrenreich, Barbara, and Deidre English. *Witches, Midwives and Nurses: A History of Women Healers*. Old Westbury, N.Y.: The Feminist Press, 1973.

Grimm, Jacob. *Teutonic Mythology*. Translated by J.S. Stallybrass. 4 volumes. London, 1880–1888.

Hand, Wayland, ed. *American Folk Medicine: A Symposium*. Publication of the UCLA Center for the Study of Comparative Folklore and Mythology, No 4.

———. *Magical Medicine: The Folkloric Component of Medicine in the Folk Belief, Custom, and Ritual of the Peoples of Europe and America: Selected Essays*. UCLA, 1980.

Hufford, David J. "Folk Healers," in *Handbook of American Folklore*. Richard Dorson, ed. Bloomington: Indiana University Press, 1986.

McClenon, James. "Supernatural Experience, Folk Belief, and Spiritual Healing, " in Barbara Walker, ed. *Out of the*

Ordinary: Folklore and the Supernatural. Logan: Utah State University Press, 1995.

O'Suilleabhain, Sean. Irish Folk Custom and Belief. Dublin: Cultural Relations Committee of Ireland, n.d.

Simboli, Cesidio Ruel. Disease-Spirits and Divine Cures among the Greeks and Romans. New York, 1921.

Utley, F.L. "The Bible of the Folk." California Folklore Quarterly. Volume IV (1964).

Wallis, Wilson D. Religion in a Primitive Society. New York: F.S. Crofts, 1929.

Zimmer, Heinrich Robert. The King and the Corpse: Tales of the Soul's Conquest of Evil. Joseph Campbell, ed. New York: Pantheon, 1948.

MAGIC AND WITCHCRAFT

Adler, Margot. Drawing Down the Moon. Boston: Beacon Press, 1981.

Buckland, Raymond. Buckland's Complete Book of Witchcraft. St. Paul, Minnesota: Llewellyn Publications, 1986.

Brand, John A. Observations of the Popular Antiquities of Great Britain: Chiefly Illustrating the Origin of Our Vulgar and Provincial Customs, Ceremonies, and Superstitions. London: Henry G. Bohm, 1795.

Budge, Sir Wallis. Egyptian Magic. New Hyde Park, NY: University Books, n.d.

Clifton, Chas. S., ed. Witchcraft Today. Llewellyn Publications: St. Paul Minnesota, 1992.

Crowther, Patricia. Lid Off the Cauldron: A Wicca Handbook. York Beach, Maine: Samuel Weiser, Inc., 1989.

Donovan, Frank. Never on a Broomstick: The True Story of the Faith, Mystery, and Magic of Witchcraft Classical and Contemporary. New York: Bell Publishing Company, 1971.

Elsworthy, Frederick Thomas. The Evil Eye. London, 1895.

Farrar, Janet and Stewart. The Witches' Way. London: Robert Hale, 1984.

200

Gardener, Gerald B. *Witchcraft Today*. Secacus, N.J.: Citadel Press, 1974.

Gifford, E.S. *The Charms of Love*. New York, 1962.

Haining, Peter. *The Anatomy of Witchcraft*. New York: Taplinger Publishing Company, 1972.

Murray, Margaret. *The God of the Witches*. London: Oxford University Press, 1970.

———. The *Witch Cult in Western Europe*. Oxford: Clarendon Press, 1921.

O'Keefe, Daniel Lawrence. *Stolen Lightning: The Social Theory of Magic*. New York: Vintage Books, 1982.

Paine, L. *Witches in Fact and Fantasy*. London, 1971.

Ryall, Rhiannon. *West Country Wicca: A Journal of the Old Religion*. Custer, Washington: Phoenix Publishing, 1989.

Seabrook, William. *Witchcraft: Its Power in the World Today*. New York: Harcourt, Brace, 1940.

Starhawk. *Dreaming the Dark: Magic, Sex, and Politics*. Boston: Beacon Press, 1982, 1988.

———. *The Spiral Dance: A Rebirth of the Ancient Religion of the Great Goddess*. San Francisco: Harper and Row, 1979.

NEW YORK STATE

Barnes, Gertrude. "Superstitions and Maxims from Duchess County, New York." *Journal of American Folklore*. Volume 36 (1923).

Benincasa, Janis, ed. *I Walked the Road Again: Great Stories from the Catskill Mountains*. Fleishmans, NY: Purple Mountain Press, 1994.

Bowman, Don. *Go Seek the Pow Wow on the Mountain and Other Indian Stories of the Sacandaga Valley*. Vaughn Ward, ed. Greenfield Center, NY: Greenfield Review Press, 1993.

Carmer, Carl. *The Screaming Ghost and Other Stories*. New York, 1956.

Dunn, Violet B., ed. "The Sacandaga Story," *Saratoga*

County Heritage. Saratoga Springs, NY: Office of the County Historian, 1974.

Gardener, Emelyn Elizabeth. *Folklore from the Schoharie Hills.* Ann Arbor: University of Michigan Press, 1937.

_____. "I Saw It." *New York Folklore Quarterly.* Vol. IV (1948).

_____. "Two Ghost Stories." *Journal of American Folklore.* Vol. LVII (1945).

Hart, Larry. *The Sacandaga Story: A Valley of Yesteryear.* Schenectady, NY: Larry Hart, 1967.

Jagendorf, M. *Upstate Downstate: Folk Stories of the Middle Atlantic States.* New York: Vanguard Press, 1949.

Johnson, Mary Ann. *Ghosts Along the Erie.* Utica, NY: North Country Books, 1995.

Jones, Louis C. *Things That Go Bump in the Night.* New York: Hill and Wang, 1959.

_____. *Three Eyes on the Past: Exploring New York Folklife.* Syracuse, NY: Syracuse University Press, 1982.

Masto, Paul. *The Great Sacandaga Lake.* Northville, NY, 1992.

McMurray, James. *The Catskill Witch and Other Tales of the Hudson Valley.* Syracuse, N.Y.: Syracuse University Press, 1974.

Pitkin, David J. *Saratoga County Ghosts.* Ballston Spa, NY: Aurora Publications, 1998.

Sawyer, Donald J. *Shoo-Fly and Other Folk Tales from Upstate.* Gloversville, NY: Mayfield Books, 1984.

Thompson, Harold W. *Body, Boots and Britches: Folktales, Ballads and Speech from Country New York.* New York: Dover Publications, 1939, 1967.

PRIMARY SOURCES

Gandee, Lee R. *Strange Experience: The Secrets of a Hexenmeister—How to Employ the Hex Signs and Spoken Spells of Rural American Folk Magic.* Englewood Cliffs, NJ: Prentice Hall, 1971.

Magnus, Albertus (1200–1250). *The Egyptian Secrets, or*

Black and White Art for Man and Beast, Revealing the Forbidden Knowledge and Mysteries of the Ancient Philosophers, n.d.

Mather, Cotton. *Christi Americana: Remarkables of the Divine Providence Among the People of New England*, 1702.

Mather, Increase. *An Essay for Recording of Illustrious Providence*, 1684.

Zall, P.M., ed. *A Hundred Merry Tales and Other Jestbooks of the Fifteenth and Sixteenth Centuries*. Lincoln, Nebraska.: Bison Books, 1963.

ABOUT DON BOWMAN

Donald Charles Herbert Douglas Bowman was born at home in Woodside, Long Island, May 27, 1911. When he was still a minor, he bought a sixty-seven acre farm at the foot of Spruce Mountain Fire Tower in the Town of Corinth, Saratoga County, New York. Bowman held many jobs clearing the Sacandaga Valley for the 1930 flooding which created the Great Sacandaga Lake:

. . . there was the *Dentist Gang*. We used jack hammers and drilled holes in the native rock below the river bed, for blasting. When I ran a wagon-drill, a promotion, they called "Doctor Don." With that machine, I could even drill horizontal holes or angle holes.

The *Barn Busters* and *Barn Buster Gangs* had names that told the story. I was also a *Powder Monkey*, tamping sticks of dynamite down in the drilled blast holes in the rock, using a long, limber, slender wooden pole . . . capping and laying wires to the detonator box. . . . They told me it was okay for me to handle the dynamite and blasting caps, that I was old enough at 17 to risk blowing myself and others to kingdom come . . . but not old enough to drive any equipment . . .

I also worked a little as a grave digger. . . . We carefully removed, tagged the remains . . . and reburied them. We were given the happy name of the *Boneyard Gang!*

[In all we cleared] nigh onto forty-two square miles of trees, brush, barns, houses, business places and such like, and had fires goin' for almost two years. [We reburied] about 2,000 bodies.

As he worked with men native to the Sacandaga Valley, Bowman says he "listened and learned." He took their stories down in notebooks and kept them for fifty years, until he sent them in letters to writer, storyteller and publisher Joseph Bruchac.

The Witch of Mad Dog Hill is the second collection of stories gleaned by Vaughn Ward from the Bowman-Bruchac correspondence. Greenfield Review Press published the first Bowman collection, *Go Seek the Pow Wow on the Mountain and Other Indian Stories of the Sacandaga Valley*, in 1993.

ABOUT VAUGHN WARD

Vaughn Ward has been chronicling and presenting Upper Hudson and Adirondack oral traditions for three decades. She is the director and founder of Black Crow Network (a not-for-profit organization dedicated to telling the region's stories from multiple perspectives), a 1999 inductee into Schenectady, New York's *Academy of Women of Achievement*, and a member of the International Womens' Writing Guild. In addition to her folklore and administrative work, she is a workshop leader, performing artist, writing coach and the proud Mama Liar of the Adirondack Liars' Club.

Ward has created five previous collections of Adirondack folklore from first-person narratives, four for Greenfield Review Press. She lives with her husband (composer, folklorist and musician George Ward) in Rexford, New York, just up the hill from the old Erie Canal. In 1998, the Wards received a rarely-given *Evergreen Award* from Traditional Arts of Upstate New York for lifetime service to North Country communities and people. They have two grown sons, Peter and Nathaniel Ward, and a granddaughter, Silas Ward.